Slippery Business
LACED UP AND SLIDING INTO LOVE

CATHY BANKS

TURBO KITTEN INDUSTRIES

To Avery for loving me without limits and never giving up on us.

CHAPTER 1

Sam

I<small>T HAD BEEN TWO YEARS SINCE</small> I <small>LEFT MY HOMETOWN TO</small> go to college and joined my dream hockey team, the Westwood Ravens. Being back was a bit surreal as so many things had changed in that short time, myself included. While I wasn't one of our star players, I was a starting player and slowly making a name for myself, scoring goals and earning my team's respect.

Coming home, I'd thought more people would recognize me, but it seemed that I wasn't that popular yet. Something to work on for sure. Not that I really wanted to be famous famous, but at least having the people in my own small hometown recognize me from playing on the hockey team would be nice.

Skating out onto the ice of the year-round ice rink our town had, I recalled all the times I'd spent here growing up. As I made my way around the rink, skating slow and just enjoying time on the ice that wasn't a drill or practice, I felt a sense of calm that I had not felt in years.

Around me, a dozen other people skated, most slowly and

1

poorly, but a few going fast or trying to perform tricks. There were a handful of kids, a few of them gripping the wall as their skates slipped on the ice as they tried to figure out how to balance.

One woman struggling as hard as the kids caught my eye. She had plain brown, straight hair, a black hoodie that was at least two sizes too large, and her skates were loose and her ankles wobbled a ton. When she lifted her head to blow hair out of her face, my breath caught.

Mollie West. In junior high, I'd had a crush on her that had grown even more when we were in high school. She'd been a bit overweight then, constantly wearing baggy clothes and hiding her face with the hood of her sweatshirt or her hair. While she hadn't been what most considered stunning or beautiful, I had always thought she was adorable and sweet. We'd been paired up on a class assignment and she'd worked extra hard, but anytime I tried to talk to her outside of class, she'd blushed and scurried away. My fragile ego had assumed she wasn't interested in me, but recently I'd been thinking back on those interactions and I wondered if that might have been wrong.

I'd been with quite a few women since then, had my share of puck bunny one-night stands at the college, and had since learned a few things about women. Not that I was sleeping around a lot like my team members, or that I thought I truly knew women, but I did know that looking back now, I was fairly certain Mollie had liked me, but had just been too shy to accept my attention as interest.

She was a big part of the reason I was here during break. No matter what I did, I couldn't stop thinking about her. She wasn't on social media often, so I wasn't sure what she had been up to. Her profile said she was single though.

As I skated next to her, she slipped and her arms flailed. An adorable yelp squeaked out of her lips as she started to fall.

Wrapping an arm around her waist, I spun us around on the ice, keeping us both upright. "Whoa!" I said with a soft laugh. "You okay?"

She looked up at me from beneath a curtain of hair and smiled shyly. "Thank you. I'm sorry. I've been trying to get better, but this is only my second time on the ice and I can't seem to figure it out. Maybe I should just get off the ice." She started to reach for the wall, but I shook my head, stopping her.

"How about some advice?"

She frowned. "You skate a lot?" Her head tilted a bit, her hair finally falling out of the way so I could fully look at her face. She was even more adorable than I remembered. Totally the sweet, girl-next-door vibe that I loved.

My chest hurt a bit that she didn't seem to recognize me, but I had bulked up considerably since the last time I had seen her. "Yeah, you could say that," I replied. Glancing down, I realized one of her skates was untied. "Let's get your skate tied first." Gripping her hands, I gently pulled her to the door that allowed you to enter and exit the rink.

She sat on one of the benches and reached down to tie her skate, but I grabbed the laces first.

"You've got to make sure your skates are tight, to help prevent your ankles from wobbling," I instructed.

Her silence worried me, but when I glanced up, I saw she was watching intently.

"There, are you ready to try skating again?" I stood and held my hand out.

Her lips flattened into a thin line and she asked, "Why would you help me?"

Smiling sweetly, I said, "Mollie, isn't that what friends do?"

Her eyes widened, her cheeks turned pink, and she asked, "Wait, you know me? Wh-Who are you?"

CHAPTER 2

Mollie

THE HANDSOME STRANGER WHO HAD RESCUED ME FROM another fall and hurt bum, continued to smile at me as I asked how he knew me.

There was no way this hot guy was friends with me. I would remember that.

"I suppose it has been a few years since we've seen each other, so I shouldn't have assumed you recognized me. I'm Sam. Sam Tucker."

My mouth dropped. Sam Tucker had been attractive in junior high and high school, but he'd definitely had a glow up these past couple of years. The kind, quiet guy I remembered didn't seem to match this man, though.

"Sam Tucker?" I asked. "The one I did the photosynthesis project with?"

His smile widened, revealing sparkling white teeth and a single dimple on his left side. "You do remember me!"

How could I forget him? He'd been really nice and actually did his part on our project, which had surprised me since he was a jock, and the other jocks I'd been paired up with only wanted to present on a project, not do the work.

"I don't want to take up your time," I said. "I am terrible at skating."

"You just need some help," he said confidently.

His hand was still outstretched, open and waiting.

I did want to learn, and being instructed by such a handsome man would be fun and a nice change of pace. Being so shy made it hard to date, and while I knew this wasn't a date, if he could help me, I could spend time with him and learn. I never had the courage to say anything before, but I had had a humongous crush on him. So bad that I'd barely been able to look at him.

Taking a breath for confidence, I set my hand in his.

Marie, my best friend, didn't understand my sudden interest in ice skating. I didn't want to admit that it was from reading a figure skating romance recently, so I refused to explain to her.

My face was definitely on fire as he led me back out onto the ice. Thankfully, there weren't very many people skating today, but I still ducked my head down, letting my hair fall over my face.

"Eyes up," Sam instructed me. "Look ahead of you, in the direction you want to go."

His hand was sturdy in mine, his body warm as he hovered just behind me.

"Just be confident, everyone falls, so don't be afraid."

Being confident was impossible for me. No matter how many self-help books I read, self-esteem seminars I watched, or positive affirmations I said, nothing helped. Not even losing weight and toning up had helped.

"Easier said than done," I whispered, but lifted my eyes so I looked ahead of me. One foot after the other, I moved slowly across the ice. Not holding onto the wall actually helped, shockingly, and Sam was very sturdy next to me. He really must skate a lot.

"There you go," he praised.

We made a full circle and a smile started to form as my confidence in skating grew. This wasn't so bad!

The little girl in front of us slipped and landed on her butt.

Due to my sudden confidence, I was going too fast and couldn't turn or stop. I was going to crash into her!

Sam slid his arm around my waist, skidded to a stop, and pulled my back against his chest. His firm, muscular arm held me up, my skates barely touching the ground.

How strong was he? Sure, I had lost weight, but he was holding me with one arm. On the ice!

My heart hammered against my chest and my face burned.

"You okay?" he asked me and gently lowered me so I could get my balance on the skates.

"Y-Yeah," I stuttered.

He waited a moment before letting me go fully and squatted down with his hand out to help the little girl. "You alright, hun?" he asked her, a warm, wide smile on his face, revealing the single dimple he had on his left cheek.

She sniffled as he helped her up and rubbing her butt. "Yes, just hurt my tailbone."

Carefully, I skated to the edge and off of the ice.

That was enough excitement for me today. I needed water.

As I untied my skates, Sam walked over.

"Thank you for helping me," I said while untying them, keeping my eyes down.

He sat down next to me and untied his skates as well. It was then I realized he wore hockey skates.

"You're welcome. I think you'll have no problem now. You were skating well until she fell in front of us."

I nodded, glad my hair was hiding my face and the blush there.

While we had known each other in school, we hadn't been friends. I'd just had an unrequited crush on him.

Even now, I could hardly look at him with how handsome he was.

"Are you single?" he asked.

My brows furrowed. What? Why was he asking that?

"Yes," I answered as I struggled with loosening one of the skates to be able to get it off.

"Would you like to get coffee or lunch?" he asked.

I blinked and stopped mid skate removal.

Turning my head, I looked over at him to see if he was talking to someone else. Looking around it was clear we were the only ones in this area.

"M-Me?" I asked.

CHAPTER 3

Sam

Her look of surprise was absolutely adorable.

"Yes, I'm asking if you, Mollie, would like to have lunch with me, Sam?" I reiterated to be more clear.

She blinked three times quickly and her cheeks turned a deeper shade of red. "O-Okay."

I smiled wide. "Great!"

We finished changing out of our skates and into shoes and I couldn't stop smiling at her red face and the way she kept letting her hair cover it.

Just like old times.

She turned in the skates and grabbed a small bag from one of the lockers while I put my skates in my backpack and put it on my back.

With one hand gripping her other elbow, she walked over to me, her eyes darting to mine, but then quickly dropping to the floor.

I pushed open the door to exit the building and asked, "Do you still like pasta? I haven't stopped in at Lucy's Ristorante yet."

She paused a second before stepping out past me. "Um, I don't really eat pasta anymore, but I can eat at Lucy's still. She knows my preferred meal."

She didn't eat pasta anymore? She used to always eat pasta for lunch at school.

Outside, the heat immediately smacked us in the face. It was such a drastic difference from the skating rink, which was kept cold to keep the ice cold.

Mollie huffed and pulled her sweatshirt off over her head. "I hate how hot it's been lately."

My eyes widened as her tank top was exposed, revealing toned arms and a narrow waist. I'd noticed it when I had grabbed her earlier and held her, that she was light, but I hadn't thought she would be so toned. As a devout gym goer, I wanted to ask her to flex, but judging by the way she was still acting like she had in high school, I was fairly certain that would make her embarrassed and I didn't want to scare her away.

"It does seem to be a bit too hot since it's only April," I agreed, turning away so she wouldn't catch me ogling her.

We walked the two blocks in silence, but I didn't mind. It was nice to walk around my hometown. It had been small before, a population of two hundred, and now it was a whopping five hundred. My mom complained about how big it was, which just made me smile. She had no idea what it was like living in a truly large city. I knew for certain she would hate it.

Small towns had a certain charm to them. People were friendly here, smiling and waving to you even if they didn't know you. They would help you if your car broke down, offer you food if you looked hungry, and looked out for each other.

It was a nice environment, but I'd felt stifled and bored, which was why I'd moved out of state for college.

I opened the restaurant door and smiled at the familiar setting. This restaurant had been here for forty years, but when her parents couldn't run it anymore, Lucy had taken over, changing the menu, but keeping the décor.

Lucy looked up from where she stood at the check-in counter and smiled at Mollie. "Hey, Mol. Did you finish the book I lent you?"

Mollie nodded. "I'll return it to you tomorrow. I, uh, didn't know I'd be coming here today."

Lucy looked at me and her eyes widened.

"Hi, Lucy."

She squealed and ran around to hug me. "Sam! I thought you weren't coming until next week."

I hugged her back and laughed at her excitement. "Yeah, well, who could wait to come back here."

Mollie scoffed, but was heading to a booth on the side of the restaurant by the windows so I didn't get to see her face.

"You here with Mollie?" Lucy asked in a shocked whisper.

"Yeah, I invited her to eat with me. Don't be spreading rumors, though."

Lucy rolled her eyes. "Sam, there are three founders in here, you think I'm the one you need to worry about spreading rumors?"

Looking around, I noticed the table with the three old women. They were from the town's founding families and the worst gossipers in existence. It wouldn't even be nightfall before the entire town heard I had come here and eaten with Mollie.

"Well, I've never been afraid of the limelight before, so I guess I won't be starting now."

It was Mollie I was worried about.

"Why are you here with her? No offense, but she's not your normal crowd and I know that little wallflower didn't put the moves on you." Lucy looked over at Mollie, who had taken a seat and was reading over the menu. She looked back at me and said, "Don't you hurt that girl or I'll kill you. She's not a conquest to be had, you understand? You may be my friend, but I won't hesitate when it comes to her."

"It's good to hear she has friends like you at her back." I patted her shoulder and walked over to sit across from Mollie.

"If you'd rather eat with Lucy –" Mollie whispered as she continued to look at the menu, despite likely already having it memorized.

"If I'd rather eat with Lucy I would have just come here and not asked you," I said quickly.

She canted her head as she looked up at me.

It had only been two years, but somehow, she had changed from cute to pretty – no, beautiful. Her eyes sparkled with curiosity.

"So, tell me what you've been up to since graduation?" I asked.

"Not much, just working and reading and stuff," she said.

"What do you do for work?"

She tensed a moment then said, "I'm a librarian."

I smiled. "That's awesome. I know you said you wanted to become a librarian in junior high."

Her eyes widened. "You remember that?"

I reminded her, "We had to do a presentation on our planned careers, remember?"

She frowned a moment then asked, "So, did you become a doctor?"

Laughing I shook my head, "No, I'd only done that as my presentation since it was so easy to find pictures for the PowerPoint."

She smiled and shook her head. "I bet a lot of those presentations were done that way. I really can't see Charlie Beckford becoming a dentist."

"Actually, he is training to become a dentist," I advised her.

Her eyes widened and mouth popped open. "No way!"

I nodded. "He's at the same college as me."

Now that I thought about it, I was surprised she didn't go to college, or maybe she just went to a local one.

"Well, I guess looks can be deceiving," she said.

"So, Ms. Librarian, what's the latest drama in Smithston? Catch me up."

She smiled and asked, "How much time do you have? You've been gone two years, so there's a lot of tea."

I pushed my empty glass towards her and said, "Fill 'er up."

CHAPTER 4

Mollie

I WASN'T SURE WHAT SAM WAS DOING TALKING TO ME OF all people, but when he talked to me, he focused on me like I was the only one in the room.

It made me want to keep his attention on me for as long as I could. Plus, I couldn't remember the last time I had felt so at ease with a man.

Maybe it was from our time working on the science project together.

Or maybe it was just Sam. He had always had a large friend group.

"You remember Katie Holloway?" I asked.

He nodded. "Bright red hair and a fiery temper to match. Was a cheerleader."

"She's a roller derby champion."

His eyes widened. "Roller derby? Really?"

It had surprised us all, but she was great at it.

"Yep, and she married Misty Jennings."

"Misty? The captain of the women's wrestling club?"

I nodded. "The very same."

"Are you guys ready to order?" Lucy asked. She looked at me. "You want your usual?"

I nodded. "Yes, please." I didn't eat here often, but when I did, Lucy let me order off the menu since I tried to avoid carbs.

"Only for you, Mol. What would you like, Sam?"

"Fettuccini alfredo with chicken, hold the broccoli. Just water with lemon to drink."

Lucy nodded and spun on her heel. "Coming right up."

"Still not eating broccoli?" I asked with a smirk.

He leaned back in the seat, draping an arm across the back of the booth. "You remember I hate broccoli, huh?"

"Well, you did cause a food fight over it, so it's pretty hard to forget," I said and felt my face heat as I almost gave away that I knew quite a bit about him, since I'd had a crush on him.

He laughed. "I forgot about that."

Looking out the window, I realized there were several women our age looking in at us, talking and taking pictures.

"Uh, does your mom not know you're back now, or are you famous or something?" I asked nervously and turned away from the window, letting my hair cover that side of my face.

"What?" he asked and looked outside. He frowned when he saw the girls. "Oh. They're probably fans."

"Fans?" I asked. "What, are you a rockstar or something?" I remembered Lucy saying something about him, but not specifically what he did.

"I'm a hockey player for the Westwood Ravens," he admitted.

The Westwood Ravens were one of the more popular

college hockey teams. Dad had watched all of their games when I was growing up. I knew several from here had dreams of joining the team, but I'd had no idea that someone from our town actually had.

"Wow, that's awesome. Congratulations." Realization hit me and my mouth dropped. "When I asked if you skate often you said, 'you could say that.' You're a hockey player!" Now I felt stupid. "You didn't have to help me or take me to lunch." My face burned and I looked down at my clenched hands in my lap. What was I even doing eating with him? He was handsome, a hockey player at a prestigious college, and there was no way he was interested in a small town librarian. I'd thought this was a date, but it had to just be him wanting to find out the latest town gossip.

"I don't do anything I don't want to, Mollie," he said softly.

I looked up at him. "What?"

Lucy arrived with our food and he didn't talk again until we'd both finished our meals. Though, he had looked at my chicken breast and steamed veggies oddly.

He paid before I could offer and walked with me out of the restaurant.

"Are you free tomorrow night?" he asked.

I turned, thinking he must be talking to Lucy, but once again, it was just us. "Me?"

He laughed and tucked hair behind my ear. "Yes, you, Mollie. Are you free tomorrow night to go out with me again?"

"A date?"

He smiled, showing the dimple. "Yes."

"Is this a prank show or something?" I asked looking around. "Did Marie or Lucy put you up to this?"

His phone rang and he pulled it out. "I have to answer this, but you have to answer me first. Date tomorrow night?"

"S-Sure."

He smiled wide again and said, "Great. Meet me at the gazebo at six o'clock." He hit accept on his phone and answered, "Hi, Mom. Yes, I'm on my way to the house now."

I watched him leave, shocked and uncertain.

Sam Tucker, sexy hockey player, my school crush, asked me out on a date.

"I need to call Marie," I gasped, and fumbled in my bag for my phone.

CHAPTER 5

Mollie

MARIE AND I STARED AT MY LIMITED WARDROBE WITH scowls, stressed since my date was in a few hours. "We need to go shopping."

"Won't he hear I went shopping, and won't it be obvious I'm getting an outfit for our date? Won't that be weird?" I asked. Our town was so small that there was little chance someone wouldn't see us and he wouldn't find out I had gone shopping for an outfit.

She rolled her eyes. "Sweetheart, you're overthinking this. He's not going to care if you go shopping and he definitely won't care that you bought a new outfit for your date. In fact, he'll probably be flattered. Now, get your shoes on." She spun around and headed out of my room, her long, platinum blonde hair flowing like silk.

I was always jealous of her hair, but especially when it floated like that.

Grabbing my crossbody purse, I slid flip flops on and followed her out of our house.

When Marie and I graduated, we'd moved into her

family home together, left to her by her Nana, who sadly passed away our senior year. Marie hadn't wanted to live alone and I had desperately wanted out of my parent's place, so it had been a perfect deal.

Plus, who wouldn't want to live with their best friend and have endless sleepovers?

I knew that soon I would have to move out, though, since she and Josh, her boyfriend, were getting more serious and wedding bells were in the near future once his time in the military ended. He'd made several hints about wanting to get married when he returned, I was pretty sure to give me time to find a place of my own.

Unknown to her, I had started looking at places to buy already. Thanks to us living together and the house being paid off, we didn't pay rent or a mortgage, but I did help pay for utilities and half of the property taxes. All of that, plus my frugal ways meant I had a great savings account to afford a hefty down payment on a house.

We got into her car and drove out of our small town and to the mall in the neighboring city. Since it was Sunday, there were a lot of people and it took us a while to find a parking spot.

"They really need to put a parking garage here," she grumbled.

I nodded my agreement. "Since the town put in those track homes, the population doubled." And the neighboring three cities didn't have a mall, so our choices were very limited.

"Are you going to be stubborn today or are you going to let me do my thing?" she asked as we headed inside.

Sighing loudly, I accepted my defeat from the start. "I will concede now and let you treat me as a dress-up doll."

She clapped her hands together and smiled wide. "Wonderful."

Marie had great fashion taste and since I wanted to be my best self in front of Sam, I was grateful for her help. If it were up to me, I would wear tank tops and jean shorts year-round.

While she walked around the store picking out items for me to try on, I headed to the dressing room to wait.

"Mollie?" a familiar female voice asked.

I turned and smiled at Jessica, a girl who had lived two doors down from me as we grew up. "Hey, Jess." We hugged and I looked at her adorable summer dress and perfectly curled brown hair. "You look great."

She fluffed one side of her curls. "Thanks, I've got a date in a bit. What are you doing here? Don't you normally buy clothes online?"

I fidgeted with the end of my tank top. She was right, I mostly purchased clothes online, caring more about comfort than style.

"She's got a date," Marie informed her as she walked over carrying an armful of clothes which she transferred to me. "Go try these on and come out with each one. No hiding any of them because you're nervous about it. You already conceded, remember?"

I stuck my tongue out at her as I pushed open the curtain for the dressing room. "Yes, boss."

"A date? Who's she got a date with?" Jessica asked.

CHAPTER 6
Mollie

"THAT'S A SECRET," MARIE TEASED HER. WE BOTH KNEW Jessica could find out by the end of the night thanks to all the gossiping people in our town.

I hung up the at least one dozen outfits Marie had given me and stripped out of my clothes before trying the first dress on. It was a soft summer dress with spaghetti straps and barely went to the middle of my thighs. Flinging the curtain aside, I did a spin in the dress and waited for Marie's response.

"Maybe," she said, and waved her hand.

"Come on, give me a hint," Jessica begged. "I haven't seen Mollie let you dress her up like this since she dated that one douche."

I flinched hard and quickly took off the dress to try on the next outfit, a skirt and blouse.

The douche she mentioned had treated me like dirt, but it had taken me several months to realize it. Thankfully, he moved away so I never had to interact with him again.

"Shush," Marie hissed. "We don't discuss him."

I opened the curtain again and did a spin.

"Yes," Marie said and nodded her head. "That's definitely date worthy."

"The skirt is too short," I countered and tugged at the hem. "I'm pretty sure my butt is hanging out the back."

"It's not," Jessica and Marie said simultaneously.

"Put it in the yes pile," Marie ordered me. "And try on the next one."

"Yes, Your Majesty," I muttered and closed the curtain again.

"Marie," Jessica whined.

Marie sighed. "Fine, I'll give you one hint. Hockey."

Jessica gasped. "Sam Tucker? She's going on a date with Sam Tucker? Shut your mouth! I knew you had it in you, you sexy little librarian succubus!"

My cheeks heated and I flung the curtain open. "He asked me."

Jessica's eyes widened and Marie stood up from the couch with a smile. "He's going to ask you on a second date as soon as he sees you in that!" Jessica gasped.

"That's the one," Marie said with a nod. "This is your date outfit."

I looked at the pile still inside. "But I didn't try the others on." Turning to the mirror, I did a slow spin.

"No need," Marie said and Jessica shook her head.

"Girl, you are smokin'! All those workouts truly paid off. No guy could refuse you tonight," Jessica said with conviction. "Shit, I'm tempted to ask you out myself!"

My cheeks heated and I smoothed down the dress. "Are you sure?"

"Yes!" they both yelled.

"Then, let me change so we can get out of here."

"Next stop, Cynthia's," Marie informed me.

Changed back into my clothes, I stepped out of the dressing room and scowled at her. "No."

"You won't let me do your makeup, so we're going to Cynthia so she can do it and your hair for you."

"But –"

She put her hands on her hips. "You conceded!"

I raised my hands in surrender. "Fine." I grabbed the dress for tonight and sighed when Marie grabbed the skirt and blouse as well.

"I'm telling you, you're going to need more than one after he sees you in that dress tonight."

"You're getting my hopes up for no reason. A guy like Sam Tucker wouldn't be truly interested in a girl like me." The man was a hockey player, for goodness' sake. I'd seen hockey movies and read a few college romance books. I knew that he likely had women throwing themselves at him at college.

I didn't know why he asked me out, but I did know he was only in town for a week. So, I knew better than to get my hopes up about anything coming from this. Tonight would just be me enjoying a date with a handsome and nice man, something I rarely got to do since our town was so small.

Right. Tonight, I would have fun with the knowledge there was a zero percent chance it went anywhere from there. And I was okay with that.

CHAPTER 7

Sam

It had been quite a while since I'd cared about getting ready for a date. Most times, I just threw on a standard outfit, combed my hair, and called it good.

Tonight, I tried on three different outfits before finally deciding on one, actually styled my hair for a change, and did some pushups to get some blood flowing to my muscles for a pump. I had also sprayed on cologne, something I very rarely did.

"Where are you off to?" Mom asked as I put on my shoes and headed for the door.

"Date," I answered.

Her eyes widened. "With someone from here? Who? Lucy?"

"Mom, you know Lucy and I are just friends," I reminded her. While Lucy was attractive, I didn't have feelings for her like that.

"Is it someone from college? Did you bring a girl home?" she asked hopefully.

"I'll be back late, Mom. Don't wait up."

She huffed. "You know I'll get a call as soon as you're spotted. I don't know why you think you can keep a secret. You haven't been gone from this town that long."

I kissed her cheek and said, "And I know you can't stand the suspense, but I'm going to enjoy my night knowing you are waiting by the phone for one of the gossipers."

"Brat!" she called after me as I shut the door and headed down the street.

Since we only lived two blocks from the town center, there was no reason for me to drive.

People waved and greeted me as I walked down the sidewalk, but I mostly kept my head down, not wanting them to try to pull me into a conversation and make me late. The last thing I wanted to do was be late and potentially make Mollie think I was standing her up.

I got to the gazebo, a wooden structure where the town held events and those who stayed here got married. It had been repaired dozens of times over the decades and was listed as a historical site.

Standing in the center, looking down at her phone, was a beautiful woman with a ponytail full of curled hair, muscular legs, and a stunning, form fitting pink dress. I had never seen Mollie dressed up before and it had me stopping in place.

She turned and spotted me, her eyes widening a bit as she looked me over.

A smug smile tilted up my lips as I walked up to her, noticing the way she looked at my dress shirt sleeves rolled up to expose my forearms. It was well-known that women liked when men rolled up the sleeves of their shirt to show off muscular forearms, and while I didn't particular focus on them, I had nice arms thanks to hockey.

"You look beautiful," I complimented as I walked up the steps of the gazebo to her.

She blushed and smiled nervously. "Thank you. You look, um, nice too."

"Hot?" I offered.

Her lips twitched. "Yes, that was what I was thinking." She laughed and rubbed her arms. "Sorry, I'm not really used to this."

"Talking to a man as hot as me?" I asked.

"Dating," she said, though I could see her shoulders had relaxed at my joke.

"Don't worry, I won't bite," I promised. "That's reserved for third dates." I winked at her and smiled wider as she blushed again.

"You're an awful tease, you know that?" she said and headed towards the steps of the gazebo.

"Wait," I said and gently grabbed her arm.

She stopped and looked at me over her shoulder. "Huh?"

Pulling my phone out of my pocket, I set it on the rail of the gazebo in front of us, glad I had a phone that could fold in half so I could set it up and take a photo. "We need to take a photo to commemorate our date."

She scowled, but stepped back into the center of the gazebo.

After setting the timer, I hurried next to her, sliding my arm around her waist and tucking her close against my side.

"Say 'cheese,'" I said.

"Cheese," she said at the same time as me, just as the camera flashed multiple times.

She blinked a few times. "Was that more than one photo?"

I nodded and grabbed my phone, opening the photos to show her. The first image she looked a little stiff, but the next couple, her face softened into a real smile. She looked amazing and I was definitely saving them.

"Oh," she whispered. "Those aren't half bad. I usually don't take pictures well."

"Hence the multi-shot," I explained. "I can send them to you, if you want?"

She nodded and smiled. "Yes, please. Then I can tell everyone I went on a date with the famous Sam Tucker."

Hearing her call me famous made me happier than it should have since she was partially kidding, but I held onto that feeling.

"Can I have your number?" I asked and held out my phone with a new contact open.

She looked up at me and asked, "Aren't you supposed to ask for it *after* our date? What if it doesn't go well?"

"If it doesn't go well, it'll be because I screwed up somehow and I'll need your number to text and call to apologize."

Her eyes widened and she took the phone to enter her number. "You're really something. I swear, you sound just like the main character from a book I read recently."

"Oh, have you been reading hockey romance? Gearing up for our date?"

Her cheeks flushed. "No."

She definitely had read it before.

"Your secret is safe with me."

Huffing out a breath, she handed me back my phone and said, "It was a figure skating romance, not hockey."

My eyes widened. "That's why you were skating?"

"Yes, but I'll deny it to my dying breath if you tell anyone else," she said and skipped down the gazebo steps.

CHAPTER 8

Mollie

Sam Tucker was ... confusing.

He took me to dinner at Brickhouse for steak and then to the bar next door. The entire time, he asked about me and my hobbies. People tried to talk to him, but he asked them to catch up later since he was on a date, focusing completely on me.

Not once did he look at any of the gorgeous girls in the bar as we played darts and drank. He even turned down Felicia who had snuck over while I was headed to the bathroom to ask him to leave with her.

People rarely turned Felicia down.

It didn't make sense.

"When are you going skating again?" he asked as we waited for our next round of drinks.

This would have to be my last round, since I was already tipsy and didn't want to get stupid drunk.

"Um, tomorrow after work."

"What time?" he asked.

"I get off at four," I answered. Did he want to go again?

"Mind if I join you?"

"Oh, you really don't have to help me again," I said and shook my hands at him in front of my chest.

"I like skating, and skating with you sounds more fun than skating alone," he said as he paid for our drinks.

Brandon, the bartender, looked at me oddly.

"What?" I asked him. We'd known each other our whole lives, like most of the people in the bar.

"What are you doing with him?" he asked.

"Why Brandon, are you jealous?" Sam asked.

I scoffed. "He's not jealous. He probably thinks you're crazy for staying with me instead of leaving with Felicia." Brandon was known to sneak off with her.

"Sweetheart, there are a million Felicias in the world, but there's only one you," Sam said and kissed my cheek. He grabbed the drinks and headed back to the high-top table we'd been sitting at.

"Careful with that one, Mollie," Brandon whispered.

I laughed and fanned my face. "Don't worry, Brandon. He's just here a few days and seems like he wanted someone easy to hang out with." All my life that's what I had been told. *You're so easy to hang out with. Like a sister I never knew I had.* All while I'd wished to be more.

He shook his head and walked away to help another customer.

"Let's make a bet," Sam said when I sat next to him.

"A bet?" I asked. "I don't like bets."

"This is a friendly bet," he said. "If I win the next game of darts, you have to come watch me play one game next season."

Going to watch a game in person had always sounded

34

fun, but I hadn't wanted to go by myself and it was a long trip.

"What if I win?" I asked.

"What would you like?" he asked.

Honestly? I hadn't thought about it yet.

"If I win, you have to get me and Marie the best seats in the stadium, and introduce us to Jackson Porter." Jackson Porter was the captain of the Westwood Ravens and insanely hot. Plus, Marie had a huge crush on him, so if we could get her a signed jersey, she'd die.

Sam frowned. "Porter? Why him?"

"I want to get an autograph," I said with a shrug.

"So, if I win, you'll come see one of my games and if you win, you'll come see one of my games?" he asked.

"Well, in one scenario I pay for the seats and in the other, you pay and have to introduce me to your captain," I said.

"You could just ask me to get you an autograph, you know?"

Did I know that?

"Do you want me to change my terms?" I asked. "If you really don't want to introduce me to Porter—"

Honestly, I didn't understand why he was against it. Was he embarrassed for me to meet Porter and potentially tell him we had gone on a date?

"Deal. Let's play," he said, took a big drink of his beer, and headed to the dart board.

CHAPTER 9

Sam

I KNEW THAT A LOT OF WOMEN WERE INTO PORTER, BUT hearing Mollie ask to meet him irrationally upset me.

I was going to win this bet, though, so I could get her to one of my games.

That was all I cared about, even if I did have to get an autograph from him. I'd just make it clear upfront that she was with me. To prevent any issues. We had a rule about not going after each other's girls and I knew he'd respect it.

"How are we playing?" Mollie asked, sipping on her drink. After having a couple of drinks, she'd finally loosened up a bit and relaxed around me. I hoped the more time we spent together, the more she'd act like this.

"Three darts each. Highest score wins," I said.

She hopped off the chair and wobbled a bit, but smoothed down her dress and walked up to grab her darts. "Sounds good."

"Ladies first," I said and backed up a bit to give her room.

"Can I ask you a question?" she asked as she aimed and threw her first dart.

My eyes widened as it hit the bullseye.

"Yeah."

"Why do you want me to come watch one of your games?"

I stepped up next to her and threw my dart, hitting the outer bullseye.

"Because I'd like to see you in the stands while I'm playing," I admitted.

Her brows furrowed and she aimed for her next throw. "Me?" she asked it so softly I was pretty sure she didn't mean for me to hear. She threw the dart, hitting the center bullseye again.

Had she been toying with me during the games earlier? Was she a darts shark?

"Yeah," I answered and threw my next dart, finally hitting the center bullseye.

She stood still, staring at the dart board silently. After a long pause, she turned and asked, "Are you actually attracted to me? Is this a date date?"

My brows furrowed. "What? What do you mean? Of course this is a date? Is there another type?"

She walked over to the table and slowly drained the rest of her beer.

What was going on in her head? Did she really not think I was attracted to her? Why else would I ask her on a date? I knew she had been self-conscious before, but was slightly baffled by this response.

Drink empty, she set it down, picked her dart back up, and walked over to stand next to me again, eyes focused on the dart board.

With a deep breath, she aimed, but I could see her hand

shaking slightly. She tried another deep breath and threw the dart. It hit the triple twenty.

My eyes widened. She was definitely a shark.

I set my dart down and laughed softly. "I guess I'll be paying and introducing you to my captain."

She walked up to the bar and waved Brandon down, getting both a water and another drink.

Her cheeks were bright red and I had a feeling it wasn't just the alcohol making her blush so deeply.

I felt certain my guess was now fact. Mollie was interested in me.

Brandon and Mollie were arguing about something, so I walked up to them.

"Don't make me call Marie," Brandon threatened her.

"What's going on?" I asked.

"He's being ridiculous," she huffed and chugged the glass of water. "Fine, be that way, Brandon." Turning to me, she smiled and said, "I had fun tonight and I expect to have the best seat ever. I'll see you tomorrow. Night."

With a quick spin, she grabbed her purse and headed out of the bar.

CHAPTER 10
Sam

"WHAT DID YOU SAY TO HER?" I DEMANDED FROM Brandon.

"I told her she couldn't drink anymore. I know you've been away at college with people who can handle their liquor, or who don't care if they can or not, but that's not how it works here. Mollie has a bad habit of turning into a sobbing mess when she drinks, or falling asleep at the park and scaring Marie half to death when she doesn't come home."

"Shit," I whispered and pulled out cash to pay for the drinks. "I'm going after her."

"She'll be headed to Ma's convenience for more drinks and to the swings in the park," he yelled after me.

Running outside, I looked around, trying to spot her, but couldn't find her. With a sigh, I headed towards the park and the swings. While I didn't particularly enjoy dealing with emotional women, I wasn't about to let her drink by herself because I'd embarrassed her somehow or let her sleep in the park.

I got to the park and scowled at the lack of lighting. They really needed to install lights.

The closer to the swings I got, the louder I could hear a woman singing. I didn't recognize the song, but I knew the voice.

Mollie.

"You left our date to come swing?" I asked and sat on the empty swing next to hers.

She frowned. "Brandon, that bastard."

"He was worried about you. Was I so bad of a date?"

Closing her eyes, she leaned back to swing higher. "It's not you. I had a lot of fun on our date."

"If you don't want to come to a game, you don't—"

"I want to go to the game. I just needed a breather," she said quickly. "I ... I haven't been on a date in a while and the last guy was a piece of work. I thought you were just going out with me because I'm easy to be around."

"I mean, you are easy to be around, but—"

She interrupted me, kicking her legs harder to swing herself higher, eyes closed and head tilted back slightly. "That's what several others told me before. I'm easy to be around, so it made sense to ask me on a date. Or, I was fun to date, but not girlfriend material. It made me want to stop dating for a while," she answered and huffed out a breath. "Look, I'm going to be honest. I'm not good at this. I am not the type of girl you're used to dating."

"You don't know who I'm used to dating," I countered.

She opened her eyes and said, "Oh, well, I guess that's true. I don't know what you've been up to in the last two years, or how many girls you've dated, or how many girl-friends you have had."

"Mollie, it's really simple, okay? Did you have fun tonight?" I asked.

She nodded and stopped swinging.

"Do you want to do it again?"

She nodded again and tipped her head down slightly to hide her face.

"Then, let me walk you home tonight, and tomorrow I'll see you for skating practice and take you out for dinner afterwards. Okay?"

She opened her eyes and looked at me, a curious expression on her face. "And what happens when you go back to college in a few days? You forget this ever happened?"

"I definitely won't forget this happened. Plus, you'll be coming to see me, remember?"

"Sam—"

"Let's worry about the future as it comes. My philosophy is to enjoy the here and now. So ..." I stood off the swing and held my hand out to her. "Can I walk you home, Mollie?"

She nodded and set her hand in mine. "Sure."

CHAPTER 11

Mollie

My phone pinged, alerting me to a message.

ST: How's skating practice going?

Me: Great! I was able to do a stop just like you showed me and I did the salchow!

ST: How bruised is your butt?

Me: No comment 😶

ST: lol 😊

It had been two months since Sam had gone back to college. Every day he texted me. Every night he called me. Most times our conversations were short and simple, but it made me happy to know he still wanted to talk.

He had even convinced his mom to bake me cookies, which had been really awkward to accept. She'd just smiled and forced me to take them.

ST: How would you feel about taking 🛼 lessons?

Me: You already give me lessons 😏

ST: Not me, but a figure skating instructor

Me: ??

ST: I know you want to learn. She's not very expensive. I can get you a discount by giving her some signed jerseys.

Me: Where is she?

Was this a girl he knew? Dated?

ST: She teaches at my rink. You could stay with me so $0 rent or hotel.

Me: I have work.

ST: Couldn't you take a vacation? She does 4-day camps. You could come on Monday, stay through Thursday for the class, then stay the weekend with me 🤍

While it did sound fun, I wasn't sure there was much reason to do a figure skating camp. I had only recently learned to skate after all, and while I was improving at a decent pace, or what I felt was decent, that didn't mean I was ready.

Me: I'm not sure I'm ready for a camp. 😬

ST: The next one is in one month and it's for newer skaters. Just … think about it.

> Me: If you want me to come visit you, just say so 😬

Not even a second later he texted back.

> ST: I want you to come visit me 😳

My mouth dropped. I had been joking.

> ST: Close your mouth and accept 😅

I looked around. Could he see me?

> ST: How about just a weekend? You can check out the rink, the campus, and I'll even give you your promised intro to Cap 🏒

That was really tempting. Plus, the library was going to be closed over the weekend for floor repair.

> Me: Are you allowed to have girls stay over?

> ST: I live in my own apartment.

Right, I'd forgotten he didn't stay on campus in the dorms or with his teammates.

> Me: Let me see how much flights are.

> ST: When can you come?

> Me: Friday night. I have to be back Sunday night.

> ST: Give me 5 mins 👍😏

47

What was he doing? While I waited for him, I looked up flights and double-checked my bank account.

I really did want to do the camp. It sounded like it would be fun.

My laptop pinged, so I opened it to see what email I'd received.

Staring in shock, I immediately called Sam.

He answered on the first ring. "Hello, beautiful."

"Did you just buy me plane tickets?"

"Yes."

"Sam—"

"I invited you, so it's only proper that I pay. Just like when we go on dates."

We'd set a rule that whoever asked for the date paid. It made it easier to split the costs.

Sighing loudly, I lay back on my bed and closed my eyes.

"They're non-refundable. You can't say no," he said in a smug tone. He was so proud of himself right now.

"Brat."

"I promise you'll have fun."

Honestly, I was really worried about being seen on campus by the girls that frequented his games. He had a fan club, and they were intense in the videos I had seen and the forums I read.

"Well, since they're non-refundable, I guess there's not much I can do except come."

"Yes!" he shouted.

I laughed at the excitement.

"Is there anything special I need to pack?"

"A good attitude?"

I scoffed. "You're out of luck there, buddy."

We both laughed and I tried to keep the laughter instead of the anxiety growing.

"That sexy dress you wore on our first date?" he said. "Or a similar one."

"Oh, are you going to take me on a date?"

"Duh."

"People might get the wrong impression," I said softly.

"Wrong impression? What wrong impression? That I'm dating you? Hate to break it to you, girl, but we are dating."

"Isn't that going to upset your fans?"

"You're not the first girl I've dated, hun. Plus, it's not up to my fans what I do with my personal life. I'm a hockey player, not an idol."

"Should I bring my skates?" I'd finally purchased my own pair of skates because it was cheaper in the long run than renting them.

"Yes."

"Anything else?"

He hummed a minute and finally said, "A bathing suit."

"A ... what?"

"Bathing suit. Bikini. Swimming outfit. So, we can go swimming together."

I gnawed on my lower lip nervously.

"Darlin', there's absolutely nothing to be embarrassed about. You've got a smokin' hot body. You're as toned as me, just not as muscular."

He wasn't wrong. I was really toned, but I still had a hard time showing off my body. Body dysmorphia was a real bitch. And he had only seen me in clothes, not out of them. While I knew a lot of people sexted, I wasn't quite there yet. At least not yet with him.

"Okay."

"Oh, will you bring cookies from Ma? She said she'll give you a tin to bring."

"S-Sure."

"It's only awkward because you think it is. She loves you and keeps pestering me to just marry you already, so stop fretting."

"That makes it worse," I gasped and put my face in my hands, likely red as a tomato.

"Babe, it's been months already."

"Yeah, but I'm not even ..." I didn't want to bring it up, especially not over the phone. I knew some guys weren't interested in labels and such, so I didn't want to force him. It would have been nice to know where we stood, though.

"You're not what?"

"Nothing. I need to go. Thank you for the tickets, I'll see you in two days."

"Hey!" he shouted, but I hung up before he could try to convince me to say more.

I wasn't naïve enough to think there wasn't a possibility he was dating other girls on campus as well. We didn't have a label and hadn't officially become anything, which meant he was still on the market and could date others.

That wasn't something I was going to do, but I wasn't going to be upset with him for it. Besides, how could we be exclusive when we were so far apart? Long distance relationships rarely worked.

Opening my bedroom door, I startled Marie, who'd been watching a show in the living room. "I need to go shopping tomorrow and you're coming."

Her eyes widened. "Shopping?"

"I'm going to stay the weekend with Sam. I need a bikini and a date outfit and clothes fit to be worn around campus as the girl he's dating."

Her hands flew to her mouth and she squealed. "Yes! Oh, girl! I am going to find the perfect outfits for you." She squealed again. "I'm so excited!"

CHAPTER 12

Sam

IT FELT LIKE THREE YEARS PASSED AS I WAITED TWO DAYS to go by for Mollie to arrive. Coach and Cap had noticed and made me do extra workouts.

Thankfully, it was still off-season, so I didn't have to worry about focusing on games or worry about hurting the team.

Standing in the airport, I had a hat and sunglasses on and my jacket up high to try to hide. While I didn't mind getting noticed or taking pictures with fans, today was about Mollie, and I didn't want her to feel like a third wheel.

She'd refused to tell me what had been bothering her, no matter how many times I had asked.

So, I was going to do my best to make her happy while she was here. To make her trip the best one possible.

And to show her a bit of my life.

She stepped out of the security area wearing a baggy sweatshirt and shorts, a backpack on, carrying a blanket, and dragging a suitcase designed to look like a bookshelf.

The suitcase made me smile even wider. Of course my sexy little librarian would have a bookshelf backpack.

When she saw me, her scowl disappeared as she smiled wide and blushed simultaneously.

Instead of running up and hugging her like I wanted, I waited until she got to me before wrapping my arms around her, lifting her up, and spinning her in a circle.

She squealed and laughed.

"Hello, beautiful."

"Hello, handsome. Did you miss me? I think you missed me."

As I lowered her, I pressed a kiss to her cheek. "I missed you." Her eyes widened at the kiss since it was the first time I had kissed her face so far. I planned to have more first kisses this weekend. Looking at her blanket, I asked, "Did you forget my cookies?"

She patted her backpack's shoulder strap. "Inside." After a second, she asked, "Why are you dressed like that? Are ... are you hiding?"

Shit, she probably thought I was embarrassed to be seen with her.

"I'll take it off once we're in the car. I didn't want my fans to bombard you as soon as you arrived."

She nodded, but her head dropped and her hair covered half of her face, giving away that she didn't fully believe me.

I reached for her hand, but she grabbed her suitcase and started walking ahead of me. "Where did you park?"

I led the way and she continued to look at the ground, only looking up through the veil of hair.

"How does tacos sound for dinner?" I asked.

"Okay."

Grabbing her arm, I pulled her to a stop and pushed her hair back out of her face, forcing her to look at me. "Hey."

"What?" she asked with a frown.

Taking my hat and glasses off, I smiled down at her. "Stop those negative thoughts." I poked the center of her forehead. "I really only wore these so fans wouldn't bombard us and make you anxious as soon as you got off the plane. I'm not hiding to prevent people from seeing us together."

Her eyes widened and she tried to duck her head again, but I cupped her cheeks, rubbing my thumbs over the red spots, and held her gaze. "Understand?"

She blew out a breath. "Yes."

I pressed a quick kiss to her lips, enjoying the shocked gasp, and grabbed her suitcase. "Good. Now, let's go. I'm starving!"

As we exited the airport and entered the parking garage, a woman with a camera immediately snapped some pictures.

It was crazy to me how there were paparazzi even for college athletes, even on off season.

Thankfully, Mollie didn't notice.

If I could, I would shield her from the craziness that surrounded dating an athlete. I wasn't going to *not* date her, but I would do what I could to ease her into the life.

CHAPTER 13

Mollie

APPARENTLY, I WAS AN OPEN BOOK TO SAM. HE KNEW immediately why I'd reacted to his appearance the way I had. I needed to get better at having a poker face.

His kisses had surprised me the most, though, I wasn't against it. In fact, I was a little disappointed at how chaste they were.

The plane had been cold, which was why I had the hoodie and blanket, but now, I took the hoodie off and exhaled a relieved breath. "It's so hot here."

He nodded. "Humid and hot. A deadly combo." He had taken his jacket off when we got to the car, revealing a t-shirt that showed off his muscular arms and chest.

"So, what's on our agenda?" I asked.

"Well, first dinner. Then, there's a party at Cap's house that I wanted to drop in at."

I tensed and he immediately added, "We will stay only as long as you want. We can walk in, say hi, and leave if you want."

Exhaling, I asked, "What about tomorrow?"

"Tomorrow, we're going to tour the college, get some skating in, and go to a friend's house for a pool party."

A pool party? That's why he wanted me to bring a swimsuit. I'd thought it would just be or us going to a beach or something.

"You're stressing over nothing," he sang. "It's just a few friends, not a crazy college pool party."

"You're really pushing my limits this weekend, aren't you?"

"Well, I've got to get you used to it."

"Why?" I asked with a frown. It wasn't like I could visit often. Tickets were expensive.

"Did Little Jonathan return the books?" he asked, changing the subject.

"Yes, and paid me his ten-cent fine," I said. "And apologized twice."

"Good! See, I told you he just needed some tough love."

What he'd told me was to scare him into returning the books.

Arriving at the restaurant, he opened my door for me and draped an arm around my shoulders as we walked inside.

Several people looked up, and many of their eyes widened when they saw him with me.

One of the servers waved him over. "Take whatever table you want, Tucker."

Sam raised his hand in acknowledgment and led me towards the back to a booth with low lighting and a single red candle in the center.

"Deep breath, babe," he whispered as he sat across from me.

I took a breath and fanned my face.

"I need a drink," I whispered and immediately grabbed the water the waiter brought to us, chugging half of it.

"Rough plane ride," Sam said, covering for me.

"Thank you, sorry," I said, realizing how rude I'd been.

"No worries, I'm not a fan of planes myself," the waiter, a handsome Hispanic man said. He held out his hand. "I'm Jay."

I shook his hand. "Mollie."

"I haven't seen you before, Mollie. Where'd you fly in from?"

"Stop pestering her, Jay. Can we get margaritas, no salt, nachos with beef no onions, and the fajitas, but don't worry about the tortillas, and a side of guac."

He'd remembered my favorite order.

Jay left and Sam leaned forward. "Surprised I remembered?"

"Yes," I admitted.

"Why? You remember my favorite orders."

"You know why," I muttered and picked up a chip from the basket. They were still warm!

"Because of that douche you dated," he answered and angrily bit into his chip. "If I ever see him, I'm going to knock his ass out."

"Let's hope we never see him," I said, and shook my head. "I'd rather eat a bar of soap than see him again."

Sam laughed. "Such a country girl thing to say."

"You said that exact phrase last week!"

He laughed again. "I didn't say being a country girl was a bad thing."

"I need to change before we go meet Porter."

His smile dropped. "Why? You look fine."

"I'm wearing shorts and a tank top."

"And they show off your muscular legs and arms. It looks good."

"I'm going to be there with you, I can't show up looking like this," I said and waved to myself.

"You think I'd be embarrassed to show up with you lookin' like this?"

I nodded.

"Not a chance."

"Are the other girls that are going to be there going to be dressed up?"

He sighed. "Yes."

"And you want me to show up like *this*?"

"I want you to be comfortable, so if you'd rather change, then you can change."

"How kind of you, Your Highness," I teased him.

He threw a piece of chip at me, making me laugh.

"No food fights, sir. We'll get kicked out."

Jay brought out our margaritas.

I clinked mine against Sam's. "Cheers."

"Cheers," he replied and took a drink of his.

He'd been quiet since I asked to change and I wasn't sure why.

"How crazy do your parties get?"

"Some can get pretty crazy, but this one shouldn't be too bad. They usually get the craziest after we win a game." He paused and then added, "Oh, we won't get your autograph tonight. Cap doesn't like signing during parties because it sets a precedent. We'll do that tomorrow when we go to the rink."

"Wait, he'll be at the rink, too?"

He nodded. "We're going before his practice, so we won't

interfere with his skating time, but he'll be showing up about when we leave so we can do it then."

"Okay." That put a damper on my planned outfit. I was going to wear the jersey to make it easier. I guess I'd just do that tomorrow.

A few people came over to get stuff signed by Sam, but we mostly finished our dinner in silence.

We drove to his apartment and I stared in surprise at the studio with a single bed.

Was ... Was I finally going to share a bed with him?

CHAPTER 14
Sam

SHE FROZE AS SOON AS WE STEPPED INTO MY APARTMENT, but I wasn't sure what surprised her. Last night, I'd spent an hour cleaning, so it wasn't messy or cluttered.

"I know it's small, but since I mainly use it for studying and sleeping alone –"

"It's nice," she said, turning and smiling at me. There was tension in her stance still, but she moved inside and looked at the few pictures on the desk. One was of our first date, in the gazebo. The second was me with the team. The third was me and my mom.

"If you want to shower or change, feel free. *Mi casa es su casa.*"

She opened her suitcase and pulled out a jersey.

My heart skipped a beat, wondering if she was going to wear my jersey tonight and if she knew what that meant.

Immediately my heart plummeted when I saw it was not my number, but Porter's.

"So, are you going to get the jersey signed and frame it?" I asked, trying to keep the jealousy out of my voice.

She nodded. "Then I'll wrap it up and hide it. Luckily, I only have to wait a month."

Wrap it and hide it? What? What was happening in one month?

After grabbing some clothes from her suitcase as well as a toiletries bag, she hurried into the bathroom, shutting the door and lucking it behind her.

Plopping down on the bed, I picked up the jersey and scowled at it. Why did she want this so much? Did she not understand it hurt me that she hadn't even asked for one of mine, even though we were dating? Part of me wanted to shred the damn jersey and burn it, but I took a deep breath and kept my jealousy in check.

Mollie wasn't like the puck bunnies; she wasn't using me to get to Porter. Cap was one of the best players and I admired his skill as well.

While she was here, I'd buy her one of my jerseys, then she could wear it to the game in a few months.

Her phone pinged and I realized she'd left it on the bed. It was a text message.

> Marie: You sure Sam won't mind you taking pictures of Porter shirtless and sexy at the pool party?

Really? She was going to try to get pics of Porter at the pool party? Not me? The jealousy returned, tripled in strength now. I was just as good looking and muscular as Porter. What the hell?

She stepped out of the bathroom and nervously tugged her skirt down. "Does ... does this look okay?"

Okay? She looked amazing! Her skirt was short enough it

showed off her thick, muscular thighs, but covered her butt. The top covered her chest, but showed off her stomach, revealing her ripped abs. I never thought I'd be turned on by a girl with a six-pack, but here we were.

I stood and slid my fingers along her exposed stomach. "You look sexy as fuck, Mollie."

She tossed her other clothes onto the bed and tried to duck her head, but I put my fingers under her chin and lifted her eyes back to mine.

"You look great."

"Thank you," she whispered, her voice a bit breathless.

Leaning down, I pressed my lips to hers again and was pleasantly surprised when she leaned into me, kissing me back.

Wrapping my arms around her, I pulled her close and opened my lips, sliding my tongue along hers.

She rewarded me by opening hers with a gasp and I took advantage, sliding my tongue inside and along hers.

Her hands gripped the back of my shirt and she pressed into me harder.

If I didn't stop this soon, we wouldn't make it to the party, plus, I was pretty certain Mollie wasn't ready to sleep with me yet. As much as I wanted to strip her bare and ravage her, I didn't want to scare her away.

Leaning back, breaking our kiss, a smug smile split my face as she stood there, lips parted, waiting for me to resume our kiss, a blush across her face, and her red lips swollen from our kissing.

"Are you ready to go?" I asked.

Her eyes opened fully and she nodded, trying to step back, but I held her still.

"You make it very hard to behave, Mollie. Do you know that?"

Her eyes widened a moment and then, to my utter surprise, she asked, "Who says you have to behave?"

Maybe my sweet little librarian wasn't as innocent as I had thought.

Dropping my head to her shoulder, I groaned. "While I would love to continue this, I promised Cap that I'd come tonight." I nipped her neck and said, "Maybe we'll leave the party early so we can continue this."

She turned her face and kissed my cheek. "We've got time for shenanigans later."

It took all of my willpower to step back from her and head to the bathroom. "Let me do my hair real quick." Once the door was closed, I leaned my forehead against the cold mirror and groaned. She was killing me. Taking a deep breath, adjusting myself in my pants, I focused on styling my hair quickly. I didn't want to keep her waiting. Once satisfied with my appearance, and with a little cologne sprayed on, I walked out and opened the door. "Well, we better head out."

As we drove, I noticed her touching her lips and smiling, which made me smile, too. I knew I would have to go slower when it came to her, she wasn't a puck bunny after all, but I would try to move us forward this weekend. One step at a time, and I'd successfully crossed the kissing bridge.

The house Cap and a few of the other starting lineup players lived in was a mansion owned by Cap's parents who were stupidly rich stock traders. There were seven bedrooms, a game room, pool, spa, and a kitchen fit for a king. They had converted one of the bedrooms into a theater room, too.

I parked two blocks away, the streets lined with cars for

those attending the party. The local cops would ignore us, so long as we didn't cause property damage or get too out of hand. Cap was a bit wild, but he didn't allow underage drinking or anything illegal. We had an image to maintain and a team we didn't want to get kicked off of.

The closer we walked, the louder the noise from the house grew, and the tenser Mollie got.

"I know it's loud, but I promise everyone is nice and you'll enjoy yourself," I said.

She nodded, but didn't verbally respond.

When we got to the house and she saw several groups of people on the lawn, she froze.

Reaching over, I threaded my fingers with hers and tugged her forward. "Deep breath, Mollie. I'm right here with you and I won't let anything happen to you. We just need to go in and say hi to my teammates, then we can leave. Okay?"

"No, I'm fine," she said in a shaky voice.

CHAPTER 15
Mollie

THE HOUSE WE WENT TO WAS IN FACT A MANSION. IT looked to be at least three stories with balconies that wrapped around two of them.

From the way we could hear the party two blocks away, I had known it was going to be loud and full of people, but I hadn't expected there to be *so* many people.

Everywhere I looked, there were groups. The lawn, the balconies, the living rooms, hallways ... everywhere.

As soon as he stepped inside the front door, people started calling out Sam's name and greeting him.

I got a lot of curious looks and I noticed several groups of girls whispering to each other while watching us.

The mansion was seriously impressive, and I couldn't believe people really afforded to live in these types of houses.

Sam was completely at ease as he made his way through the crowded rooms and hallways, an easy smile on his face. As much as I wanted to run away, I wanted to see and experience this with him, too. Experience him at college.

I was really glad I'd changed into the skirt outfit. All of the girls were dressed similarly.

As we passed through the kitchen, Sam grabbed two beers, popping the caps off before handing me one and continuing to lead me through the massive house.

Taking a big drink of the beer, I prayed it would help my nerves and calm my racing heart.

We entered a large living room where several couches sat filled with people. Among them were several of the main players of the team, including Jackson Porter. He sat in the center of a couch with a woman on either side of him, looking like a king.

Sam tugged me forward by our joined hands and when we stood before Porter, he draped an arm around my shoulders and said, "Hey, Cap. This is Mollie. Mollie, this is Porter, my team captain."

Jackson Porter stood from the couch and I had to tilt my head back at how tall he was. His muscles strained against his shirt and I could see why Marie had a crush on him. He smiled warmly at me and held out his hand. "It's nice to meet you, Mollie. Tucker's been telling us a lot about you."

My cheeks heated as I shook his hand. "Hopefully only good things."

He laughed. "Tucker rarely talks poorly about anyone, but I'm sure you know that as his girlfriend."

His ... what?

"He told us you're starting to learn figure skating," he commented as he sat back down.

"Uh, yeah, I'm not very good yet." I took another drink of my beer, shocked to find it was almost empty after my two drinks.

He shrugged. "We all start somewhere."

How could this superstar of an athlete be so nice?

Marie would die if she ever got to meet him.

A few of the other players introduced themselves as well as a couple of the girls.

"I think this is the first time Tucker has had a girlfriend. You must be pretty special," one of the girls on the couch opposite Porter's said. She'd been giving me dirty looks ever since she heard Porter say I was his girlfriend. Clearly, she was one of his fans or previous flings.

"She's definitely special," Sam said and slid his arm around my waist, squeezing me against his side.

"I don't know about that," I said and laughed nervously. "I'm still in shock that I'm standing here talking to the famous Westwood Ravens, honestly."

The guys and a couple of the girls laughed, but the one girl continued to glare at me.

The girl on Porter's right said, "As much as they like to think of themselves as gods, they're just men."

Porter tickled her side, making her laugh and squirm. "That's not what you were saying earlier, Brit. I distinctly remember you screaming, 'oh, god.'"

She smacked his hands away and shook her head. "The egos on these men."

My cheeks warmed at the insinuation of what they'd done earlier, but no one else seemed to care.

"Um, can we get a refill?" I asked Sam softly and shook my empty beer at him.

He nodded. "We're going to get some refills. We'll see you tomorrow, if not later."

Porter waved and smiled at me. "Have fun, Mollie."

I nodded and let Sam lead the way back to the kitchen.

"You okay?" he asked.

"Um, yeah, it's just really loud and there are so many people." It was much louder than any party or bar I'd been to before. We basically had to shout to hear each other.

He paused and asked, "Instead of getting a beer here, do you want to go somewhere else? Or get some drinks to take back to the apartment?"

"Yes," I said immediately.

The girl who'd been glaring at me came into the kitchen and asked, "Too much for you, honey? Not used to city life?"

"Tiffany, be nice," Sam ordered her.

Tiffany pouted and said, "I'm nothing but nice. You know that."

The innuendo was obvious and it made me want to hide and punch her at the same time.

Sam put his hand on my lower back and pushed me out of the kitchen. "Let's go."

"Bye, Mollie," she called sweetly.

"Ex?" I asked as we continued through the mansion.

"One-night stand," he corrected. "A huge mistake on my part. Sorry."

"Not sure why you're apologizing. Not like you cheated on me or something." Though, it did make me irrationally happy to hear him say it had been a mistake. That definitely said something about me.

"Still," he said.

We finally got into the car and I turned to face him as he started it. "Why did they call me your girlfriend?"

He frowned and turned to face me. "What?"

"You didn't correct them."

His eyes widened and he said, "Are we ... I thought ..."

"You've never called me it before or mentioned wanting to be exclusive, and so I thought you didn't want to put a label on us or anything. Or be exclusive with me, which if you still don't want that, that's fine."

He smiled and reached over to cup my cheek. "Mollie, did you think I was dating others while I was here? That I truly didn't want to be exclusive with you? Is that what you meant the other day about me buying your ticket to see me?"

"Maybe," I said and tried to turn my face away, but he kept his hand on my cheek, preventing me from hiding.

"Mollie, do you want to be exclusive with me? Will you be my girlfriend?"

CHAPTER 16

Sam

As she stared at me in silent shock, I wondered if I needed to reset her computing software.

Maybe waft a book under her nose?

How did one restart a librarian?

She blinked several times and finally replied, "Yes."

I slid my hand around her face to cup the back of her head and pulled her forward to kiss her. I gave her the longest, deepest, passion-filled kiss I could.

When I leaned back, she kept her mouth parted as she stared at me.

"No takesies-backsies," I whispered.

She laughed and kissed me hard on the mouth. "Ditto."

I drove to my apartment building, parked, and took her to the convenience store to get snacks and drinks. She spent several minutes debating over two flavors of chips, so I grabbed both and carried them to the counter.

"Sam," she gasped. "I don't—"

"We need snacks for the weekend and I eat a lot, remember?"

That explanation seemed to pacify her and she even grabbed a few more things.

I understood that she wasn't used to spending her money freely. When you lived in a small town, you were used to being frugal, and it was hard to spend excessively. Even on yourself. Thanks to my late father's investments and my scholarship, I had quite a bit of money saved up that I was more than willing to spend on her.

We headed to my apartment, treats and drinks in tow, and I found myself smiling far more than I had any previous day. Just being around Mollie made me feel relaxed and happy. She was always like that, even in high school.

"Comedy or action movie?" I asked as she set the snacks out on the coffee table and I tried to decide on a movie to watch.

"Is there one that's both?" she asked.

"There actually is," I said and started one of my favorite action comedies that I knew she hadn't watched yet. It would be my tenth time watching it, but I didn't care. I wanted to see her laugh and enjoy it as well.

All set up, I popped the top on my beer and then her own and held mine out for her to clink hers against. "To a great first weekend together," I said.

She clinked her can against mine and said, "To a great first weekend together."

As expected, she laughed out loud several times, but each time, she stopped her laugh short and covered her mouth.

That wouldn't do. I knew her ex-boyfriend had been a complete asshole, making her think less of herself, including telling her that her laugh was too loud even in the privacy of her own home when watching a movie.

I wasn't going to let that stand. I loved her laugh. I loved seeing her enjoying something and the pure joy that she let out.

When the first movie ended, I let her take the controller to choose the next one and opened our third drinks.

"Did you think any more about the camp?" I asked while I watched her.

She nodded. "I would love to do it, but I think I'm not quite ready. I think I need more practice and learning on my own first. Plus, I'm not sure I can take a full week off of work."

"Well, I think you should really consider it. Like I said, you can stay here."

She turned and looked at me fully. "Sam, I know you asked me to be exclusive earlier, to be your girlfriend, but I know how things can be at college, when you live in a completely different state from someone."

I held up my hand, stopping her.

"Movies don't always mimic real life, Mollie."

She frowned. "You've got women throwing themselves at you. I saw how Tiffany was glaring at me. If I hadn't been there, she would have been trying her hardest to warm your bed tonight."

Warm my bed? God, she was adorable! No other woman here would have phrased it that way, and I knew it was from the romance books she read. Maybe I needed to read a few and see what all the fuss was about.

"And?"

Her cheeks heated. "And, I won't be here. I'm going to be in our little town while you're here, without your needs met."

Smiling wide, I reached over and set my hand on her

upper thigh. "When was the last time your needs were met, Mollie?"

CHAPTER 17

Mollie

Did ... did he really just ask me that?

"I-I don't know," I admitted. Had they ever been met? I knew for a fact that my ex had never made me come. He had been close once, but the jerk was always about himself and he always finished first. He had never asked what I wanted, if the position was good, or what felt good.

Sure, I had taken matters into my own hands, but no man had ever done it for me.

"That's what I thought," he said as he slid his hand higher up my thigh. "You've yet to experience what a man who truly cares about you can offer. What I would be looking forward to every time we were apart, but would be willing to wait for. I've been with women, yes, but I've also been without them. I don't need to sleep with women. I can wait months between ..." he paused, "... experiences if necessary. Just because I'm a man and we won't be together for several months at a time, doesn't mean I'm going to cheat on you."

Judging by his tone, I had insulted him. I supposed I understood. If he had said the same to me, I would have felt offended he thought I couldn't keep my legs closed for such a short period of time.

"I'm sorry. I didn't mean to offend you," I said softly and rested my head on his shoulder.

"Tell me, did your ex ever make you come? Or was he always focused on his own satisfaction?"

"Himself," I admitted.

With a quick, sudden move, he had me on my back on the couch and hovered over me. "We need to fix this as soon as possible. No woman, especially no woman as amazing as you, should have yet to experience pleasure. True pleasure. The type given when a man cares and wants you to feel good."

"And that's you? You care about me feeling good?" I asked. The three drinks we'd had were definitely making me more talkative.

He leaned back and smiled at me, revealing the adorable dimple again. "Oh, darlin', I'm going to show you a whole new world."

Before I could respond, he kissed me, his tongue sliding along mine and thrusting in and out of my mouth in a way that had me panting after only a few seconds.

Pushing my shirt up, he slid his hands along my exposed skin, sending goosebumps across my body.

"Don't worry, Mollie. I'm going to be slow and easy, kind and gentle, and I'm going to worship you the way every queen deserves to be worshipped."

"I'm not a queen," I panted as he kissed my neck and nipped at my collarbone.

"You can be my queen," he whispered and stroked a thumb across one of my nipples, making my breath hitch and my hips arch. "I will be your faithful servant, here to make you happy."

He pulled his shirt off over his head, exposing all of his toned and tan muscles for my viewing pleasure.

Yeah, I could definitely be happy with this view alone.

His fingers worked quickly, removing my clothes in record speed, and while I felt embarrassed to be exposed, I let him see me.

"Utter perfection," he whispered. "You are beautiful, muscular, and everything I have ever wanted."

No man had ever said such kind words to me before. I really wasn't sure how to react.

Thankfully, I didn't need to react since he chose that moment to dive between my legs and cause all kinds of other sounds to escape my mouth instead.

CHAPTER 18

Mollie

THE RINK SAM HAD BEEN REFERRING TO WAS A STADIUM. The stadium his games were held in.

After gawking for several minutes on the tour, he convinced me to go out on the ice with him.

We skated side by side, holding hands, and despite the cold air, I felt warm inside. I lost count of the number of laps we made, but I enjoyed it more than skating alone.

"Show me your jump," he said as he released my hand.

"I'm not great at them yet," I muttered as he skated in a slow circle around me.

"I still want to see how much you have improved. If you recall, last time we skated together, you could barely get around the rink." He battled his lashes and added, "Please."

Sighing, I skated away from him to give myself space. "Fine, but only because you asked so nicely."

I would just pretend like I was on the rink back home, with people I didn't care whether they saw me fall. Since they had seen me fall a million times already.

Increasing my speed, I skated around the rink halfway,

then did my salchow. I landed nicely and smiled wide, proud of how easy it was becoming.

Keeping my momentum, I did my next jump, the toe loop.

I wobbled on my landing, but didn't fall.

Sam clapped and I realized there were other people clapping, too.

Turning, I found Jackson Porter and a woman I didn't recognize heading down the stands towards us.

Sam skated to me, picked me up by the waist, and spun us around in a circle, completely unfazed by my extra weight and the slippery ice. "That was awesome! I can't believe you've learned so much on your own."

Porter said, "That's pretty impressive, Mollie. Sam mentioned you just started learning, but you look like a natural."

My cheeks grew warm and I ducked my head. "Thanks."

"Come meet Alicia," Sam said and pulled me by my hand across the ice.

The woman, Alicia, asked, "How have you learned the jumps?"

"Watching videos," I admitted. "And recording myself to see what I look like."

Her eyes widened. "Impressive. You really should join my camp next month."

Camp? Oh! She was the figure skating coach.

I turned to Sam with a scowl. "You invited her here knowing you would convince me to jump, didn't you?"

He smiled wide. "Maybe."

Alicia held out a business card. "I know you don't live here, but I think you should really consider joining with me.

You've got talent and I think a week with me will help you improve a lot. How about this, I will offer you ten percent off the camp."

Sam's eyes widened. "You never offer discounts."

She smiled at me. "There's a first time for everything. See you next month, Mollie." She waved and walked away.

"So, Mollie. Sam said you wanted my autograph?" Porter asked where he was stretching on the bench next to us.

"Oh, yes!" I rushed to my bag, put the card in a safe place inside, and carried the jersey and pen to him.

He looked from the jersey to Sam. "You want me to sign this jersey for you?" he asked. "Are you going to wear it to our next game?"

Sam sat down and started untying his skates a serious frown creasing his brow.

"I would like you to sign it, please. It's for my best friend for her birthday. She's a huge fan."

Sam's head whipped up as he looked at me. "The jersey is for her?"

I nodded and frowned at his sudden mood shift. "Yeah, why?"

CHAPTER 19
Sam

A HUGE WEIGHT LIFTED FROM MY CHEST. SHE DIDN'T want Cap's autographed jersey for herself. She was giving it to Marie!

Cap smirked, amused by my reaction, and asked, "You sure you don't want one for yourself, too?"

If Mollie wouldn't have freaked out, I would have punched him.

"No, thank you," she replied.

Did she know what it meant for a girl to wear a player's jersey? Probably not.

He handed her the jersey and pen and asked, "Are you coming to the pool party?"

She nodded and folded the jersey carefully before putting it in her bag.

Cap stood and said, "Great. I'll see you two later then." He skated out onto the ice, beginning his warm up.

Mollie sat by me and removed her skates, a contemplative expression making her brows furrow.

"Ready for breakfast?" I asked and stood, shouldering my bag. "I am starving."

She seemed to snap out of her thoughts and looked up at me with a smile. "You're always hungry."

I flexed a bicep and said, "Got to feed these pythons."

Her eyes focused on my bicep before dropping to her skates, but I saw her lick her lips.

Last night had been great. She wasn't as experienced as some of the girls I'd been with before. However, she was willing to learn and I discovered very easy to please.

The previous jerk who'd been with her must have been terrible and super selfish.

As we ate breakfast, I noticed her eyes darting to a group of puck bunnies across the restaurant. I couldn't remember their names, but it was clear they were talking about us.

"Just ignore them, babe. It's easiest that way."

She stayed silent the rest of the meal and the drive back to my apartment.

I needed to get her out of her funk. Out of her head, where she was no doubt coming up with one thousand horrible and unlikely to happen scenarios.

After we both set our bags down, I scooped her up into my arms, smiling at her adorable screech.

I set her on the bed and cuddled her tightly in my arms. "You're going to do the camp, right?"

She rested her head on my bicep and said, "I really want to. I'll talk to the library director next week about it."

"And you'll stay with me during it?" I asked, and trailed my fingers up and down her arm.

"If you want me to," she whispered.

"I do."

Her phone beeped and she pulled it out. Curious, I looked at the screen and my eyes widened when I saw she was looking at real estate in our hometown and the neighboring cities. The email was to alert her about a new house on the market.

"One second, I need to email this to my agent to request a viewing," she said and sat up.

"You're buying a house?" She hadn't mentioned it to me at all.

She nodded. "Marie and her boyfriend are going to get married soon, so I should find my own place."

I knew it was far too soon for us to discuss living together, especially when I didn't know if I would get picked up for the NHL or not, but if she bought a house now it would be harder to convince her to move later.

"Are you sure now is the best time to buy?"

She shrugged. "Seems like a decent time. Prices aren't too crazy and interest rates are good."

"And you're sure you want to live there?"

Her head lifted and she asked, "Where else would I live?"

The words were out before I thought better of it. "You could live with me."

CHAPTER 20

Mollie

LIVE WITH SAM? WAS HE SERIOUS OR TEASING ME?

We had just become a couple. It was way too soon to live together, even if we had known each other when we were growing up. There was no way I could leave my life back home and move here. And there was no way he was going to just go back to our small town after all of this he had experienced.

"My work is there," I replied simply. After a breath I added, "And you won't be here forever. You only have two more years at the college."

"Right," he said and rubbed the back of his neck, ears slightly red. "Sorry, that was a little crazy."

Curious, I asked, "What is your plan after college?" We hadn't talked about it yet, and now seemed like as good of a time as any to find out. It was something I was insanely curious about, but hadn't broached for fear of ruining our interactions.

"Well, hopefully, the NHL will draft me. If not, then I will have to find a job using my new business degree," he answered and shrugged. "Honestly, I haven't thought about it too much yet."

I supposed that made sense. Didn't most college sports players want to get recruited for professional leagues?

"What about you?" he asked.

"Me?" I asked and frowned. "What do you mean? I'm doing it. Librarian, remember?"

"Where do you see yourself in five years?" he asked and sat up, crossing his legs to look at me better.

"At the library, owning a house of my own, growing my own food. Maybe a cute dog at my side."

"No handsome husband helping?"

I shrugged. "If that happens." The self-deprecating thought that I wasn't likely going to find anyone almost got said out loud, but I turned away and bit my tongue.

"He'd be one lucky man to wake up every day to your beautiful face," he said and set a hand on my knee, rubbing his thumb across it slowly.

"You think so?" I asked.

"I know so," he said, and nodded. Leaning over, he kissed me lightly and said, "I'm lucky I've gotten to experience as much as I have with you. That you're wasting any of your time on me."

"It's not a waste," I argued.

He smirked. "No? Well, that's good to hear. That means I must be doing something right if you're enjoying your time with me right now."

He kissed me deeply, our tongues tangling, and he pulled me onto his lap.

The niggling worries about the future kept me unable to enjoy the here and now moment with him.

Pushing back, I asked, "We should probably get dressed, right?" I stood and hurried to my suitcase to get my bikini and the shorts and tank top I was going to wear over it.

Thinking about the future made me question our current relationship even more.

If he did go pro, we would have to break up for sure. Did I want to fall for Sam only to have him taken from me in two years?

Maybe it was best to treat this like a friends with benefits situation? Enjoy our time together, but keep my heart out of it. Learn from my time with him and figure out how to behave with an insanely hot boyfriend. Figure out how to behave with a boyfriend at all for any future instances that might happen.

Yes, that's what I would do. I would let myself enjoy the time with Sam, but I would keep my heart locked up nice and tight.

Easy peasy.

CHAPTER 21

Sam

I HAD MESSED THINGS UP SERIOUSLY BAD IN JUST minutes. It was like I could see her constructing walls around herself.

Sure, she was smiling and laughing at my jokes, but there was a new tension. A separation that hadn't been there before.

I knew I shouldn't have brought up the future and my dumb ass had still done it.

When we arrived back at Cap's she relaxed a little. She even grabbed a seltzer instead of a beer when we walked through the kitchen without asking.

In the backyard, my teammates greeted us.

She smiled shyly as we set our stuff on an open set of lounge chairs. Her fingers froze as she unbuttoned her shorts.

Leaning over, I whispered, "Your body is perfect. Don't worry."

A soft exhale was my only response, but she did finish removing her shorts and shirt.

So strong. Her back muscles rippled in the sunlight as she

folded her clothes. While she wasn't bulky, she was ripped and it was surprisingly hot. Her bright pink bikini top and shorts showcased all of her muscles in the perfect way. If I could convince her, I'd get her to take pictures in the bikini on a beach for a calendar just for me.

I removed my shirt and enjoyed the slow once over she gave my exposed upper body and the slight pink that sprung up on her cheeks.

Brit whistled as Mollie climbed down the steps into the pool. "Damn, girl! You are ripped!"

Mollie blushed and quickly dove under the water.

I gave Brit a glare and she frowned. "What?"

"She's shy," I said simply before Mollie's head broke the surface.

Brit's eyes widened.

Instead of walking in like Mollie had, I jumped in next to her, causing the water to splash up over her face, making her laugh.

She floated on her back, eyes closed, enjoying the sun.

Grabbing a floaty, I lazily kicked to stay next to her. "Nice, right?"

"Yesh, she agreed. "I think my house definitely needs a pool."

A pang of hurt hit me in the chest again.

Her house. Without me.

"Mollie, what do you do for work?" Cap asked as he floated on a giant inflatable unicorn with a beer in his hand and sunglasses on.

"Librarian," she answered.

"That's hot," Paolo, one of my teammates, said.

I shot him a warning glare.

He just shrugged unapologetically.

"You like it?" Brit asked.

"I do," Mollie said. She looked over at Brit and asked, "What about you?"

"I'm still in college for another year," Brit answered.

Mollie smirked. "Right. Duh. Sorry."

Brit smiled back. "So, how often do you work out? Could you give me some pointers? I'm really wanting to work on my legs, get them more toned."

Surprisingly, Mollie swam over to hang on the ledge in front of Brit and give her tips.

"You okay?" Cap asked quietly enough Mollie wouldn't overhear.

"Yeah."

He pulled his sunglasses down and gave me a look. "Tucker."

Sighing, I admitted, "I messed up by bringing up the future. She shut down."

Sighing he said, "I know it hurts, but maybe it's for the best. She doesn't seem like the type who could handle the life of an athlete's wife. No offense meant towards her, so don't get angry."

"I know what you mean," I whispered even if I hated to admit it. "But ..."

"You like her."

I nodded.

"Maybe it's better to let her go now. Not get her hopes up."

"What if I don't go pro? What if I lose her and then have nothing?"

"That's something we all have to deal with," he said,

glancing at Brit and suddenly, I realized why she was always at his side. It wasn't just because she was his favorite puck bunny. She was his favorite.

"You've got time to make decisions. Just enjoy it for now," he said and used his hand to redirect the unicorn. "That's all any of us can do."

CHAPTER 22

Mollie

THE POOL PARTY GOT ROWDIER THE LATER AND MORE drinks everyone had. Thankfully, Sam was more than willing to leave when I asked.

Brit had asked for my number so we could text about workouts and stuff, and I agreed. It would be nice to have another friend.

Sam had been quiet most of the night and as we walked into his apartment, I broke the silence. "Would you like to watch a movie?"

He nodded. "Sure. Why don't you shower first?"

A part of me deflated, assuming he might try to convince me to shower with him, but I wasn't bold enough to request it.

"Okay."

When I come out from my shower, feeling much better, he handed me a delivery menu. "Figure out what you'd like to order while I shower, okay?"

I nodded and watched him head into the shower. How

did I fix this? Did I fix this? Was it up to me to fix this? Maybe this was for the best, right?

Yet, my chest hurt to think of us ending our weekend on such a sour note. I had to fly out early tomorrow and it would be at least a month before I saw him again.

Maybe there was one way to pull him out of his funk ...

I called the library director and requested the week off for the camp. She agreed without hesitation and said it was the perfect time for some repairs she had been putting off.

Sam was still in the shower, so I called Alicia next. "Is your offer still valid?" I asked.

Laughing, she said, "Sure is. Text me your email address and I'll send the details."

"Great!" I chirped.

Sam came out, a towel around his waist and one in his hand as he dried his hair. "What's great?"

Smiling wide, I said, "I talked to the director and called Alicia and am officially accepted to attend the skating camp. So, is your offer still on for me to stay here?"

His eyes widened and he froze mid hair drying, arm in the air. After a breath, he registered what I'd said, smiled wide, dropped the towel in his hand, and picked me up, spinning us around. "Yes! I can't wait!"

Laughing at his joy, I kissed his cheek. "Me neither."

He set me down and the smile started to wilt. "It's too bad you have to go back tomorrow."

As much as I enjoyed my time with him, I was looking forward to going back to my small, quiet town, where I wouldn't be getting glared at constantly.

He went to his room, came back wearing a pair of shorts, and headed to the fridge.

"It's only three weeks," I reminded him. "Then you'll get to see me for a full week."

"A full week?" he asked, turning with two bottles of beer in his hands.

I nodded. "I want to fly in Sunday, so I'm not jet lagged on Monday, then fly out the next Sunday so I can spend the weekend with you. If ... if that's okay?"

He set the beers on the counter, slid an arm around my waist, and pulled me flush with him. "Okay? Of course it's okay. If you wanted to stay a month I'd let you." Smirking he asked, "Does that mean you enjoyed this weekend?"

"What do you think?" I whispered, wrapped my arms around his neck, and pushed up on my toes to kiss him.

He kissed me hungrily, like it was the last time we were going to kiss, taking my breath away and making me dizzy.

His hands slid under my butt and he picked me up, setting me down on the edge of the counter, with his body between my legs, never once breaking our kiss.

When he did pull back, we both panted and sucked in air.

I stroked a hand down his muscular chest, reveling in the way his pectorals glistened after his shower.

"How did I manage to snag the attention of such a sexy man?" I asked softly, stroking my fingers across his rock hard abdominals.

"By being an adorable nerd," he answered.

Scoffing, I looked up at him to make a joke, but his face was so serious, I held my tongue.

"I'm pretty sure I fell in love with you when we did our science project together," he whispered and kissed the tip of my nose. "I was just too stupid to realize it then or realize that when you scurried away in the halls whenever I tried to talk to you, it was because you were shy, not because you didn't like me."

My eyes widened. "You thought I didn't like you?"

He nodded.

"I had the biggest crush on you and it was hard to even talk to you," I admitted. "When you would say hi, I always thought there was someone else you were talking to. That's why I ducked my head and walked off. I was scolding myself for thinking you could have possibly been talking to me."

He tsked. "We've really got to work on your self-esteem, pretty girl." He stroked a hand up my thigh and said, "Pretty sure you could choke most men out with these thick, gorgeous thighs now, and any man lucky enough to be caught would die with a smile on their face."

"Sam," I gasped and knew my face was on fire.

He slipped his fingers beneath my shirt's hem and pulled it up and over my head. "I want to watch a movie, but first, I want to watch your face as I make you scream my name."

My mouth dropped open at the dirty talk, but ... I liked it.

With a flick of his fingers, my bra clasp came undone and he threw it onto the counter behind me. "Let me show you how you should be worshipped. How anyone who is lucky enough to touch you should treat you and your beautiful body and soul."

He picked me up under the butt and carried me with ease to the bed, laying me down gently. "Tonight, I'm going to worship you until you understand how perfect you are."

CHAPTER 23
Sam

PORTER SMACKED ME UPSIDE THE BACK OF MY HELMET. "Tucker! Get your head in the game!"

"Sorry, Cap." It wasn't the first time this week that I had messed up and missed my shot.

"Tucker, off the ice," Coach ordered.

Sighing, I skated to the bench and removed my helmet.

"What's going on with you?" Martins, one of the second string asked. "You've been distracted the past few days."

"Sorry, I'll get my head back on straight," I promised.

After practice, I headed towards my car, head down.

"Tucker!" Porter called, making me stop. He caught up to me and said, "Come with me."

I didn't really feel up to socializing, but Cap seemed serious, so I knew better than to decline.

He drove us to the nearby bar, one frequented by the college sports players, and ordered us each a beer. It was still off-season, so we were allowing ourselves to enjoy before we went on a no alcohol diet for the season.

As we drank, he watched me silently.

"I'm sorry I've been distracted," I apologized, assuming that's why he had brought me here.

"What happened?" he asked.

Sighing, I ran a hand through my hair. "Nothing, I don't know. It's just, it's been two weeks since she went back home and she's been messaging less and I know part of it is because she bought a house and –"

"She bought a house? Back in your hometown?" Cap interrupted.

I nodded.

"And now your future with her is much less certain," he said.

I nodded again. "She's not flirting as much in our messages either. It's like she's –"

"Icing you out?" Cap guessed.

"When she was here, I noticed it then, at the pool party, but being apart has made it worse."

"She's coming next week, right?" he asked. "For the figure skating camp?"

I nodded.

"That explains your shitty ass playing."

My head snapped up and he smiled at me, clearly trying to get a rise out of me.

"We already talked about this, Tuck. Sure, you can enjoy your time with her, but you have to accept the possibility that you may not end up together. That it may be better to do like she is and go back to just friends."

Groaning, I ran a hand through my hair. He said it like it was so simple! He didn't know that I'd been pining for this girl for years.

"Maybe you just need to get laid," he suggested.

I glared at him. "I'm not cheating on her. That would be the worst thing I could do to Mollie."

She would never recover from that.

"I meant breakup with her and then get laid, Tucker."

Taking another long drink, I said, "I don't want to do that."

"So, what? You're going to give up on going pro?"

"I doubt I'll get signed anyway," I said.

He scoffed. "Definitely not with the way you've been playing this week." Leaning forward he said, "You've got skills and talent, Tuck. With another year or two on the team, I don't doubt you'll get signed. However, pro hockey isn't for everyone. If you don't want to go pro, don't, but don't give up on your dreams just for a girl who may not be the one for you anyway. You and her are nothing alike. I know she's your high school crush, the one you never admitted your feelings for, but do you really see the two of you lasting long-term? Pro or not? She's a sweet girl, would make any man in your little town the luckiest man there, but is that small town life really what you want? Didn't you leave there for a reason? Do you really want a boring life in the country with your librarian wife reading books and gardening all the time?"

He wasn't trying to be rude, but I wanted to punch him.

And yet, I understood what he was saying.

Groaning, I dropped my head and shook it. "I don't know."

"Well, you've got time to think about it and decide. Maybe it's good you two are talking less. It will give you time to determine if more distance or less is what you want. When she comes back next week, you can see how she handles life here and if she's going to be capable of being the woman you truly want. The partner you need. That's what we are all after. A partner for whatever life throws at us. Someone who will stand next to us no matter what happens. Is that Mollie? Or is this really just a fun time that you can look back on fondly later in life with a smile on your face, but understand it was never going to be your future?"

"I hear you," I said and huffed out a breath. "I'll take your advice into consideration."

As much as I didn't want to, I knew he was right. I really liked being with Mollie, I felt like I was able to truly be myself with her, not just a version of myself like I was with others.

But who knew what my future had in store for me, and who knew if she wanted any part of that.

Going pro would be awesome, but I wasn't as motivated as Cap or some of the others, so should I let that thought go? I loved playing, but it wasn't my life.

What would make me happiest? What did I want for myself in the next five years? Ten years?

The thought of her marrying someone else hurt, but she deserved to be happy and I wasn't certain that I was the one who would ultimately make her happiest. Maybe there was someone back home who would be a better fit for her? Someone who enjoyed the small town life that I had tried so hard to leave.

But would I have tried so hard to leave if I had known I could have been with her?

CHAPTER 24
Mollie

"I'M BOARDING IN TEN MINUTES," I ANSWERED SAM.

"I'll meet you at the airport," he promised. "Is there anything you want me to pick up before you land? Dinner for tonight? Snacks? Drinks?"

The last three weeks had been hectic beyond belief for me. On top of working and practicing new moves for the figure skating camp, I had spent a lot of time cleaning up and working on my new house. It was a gorgeous Victorian home, but the previous owner had been very old and hadn't been able to properly manage the house and perform the upkeep necessary.

I was exhausted from all of the scrubbing, washing, painting, and repairing I'd been doing. Thankfully, some of my neighbors helped or had family members who were helping as much as they could.

"A couple energy drinks for tomorrow and some chicken fettuccini alfredo would be great. I've been craving pasta and have slowly started incorporating it into my diet." Alicia and I had had a very lengthy discussion about carbs and their necessity in an athlete's diet.

What she had said made sense, but I was still being careful not to overdo it.

"I know the best pasta place. I'll make sure it's ready for pick up after I get you at the airport, so it'll be hot when we get back to the apartment," he promised.

"You're the best," I praised.

We hadn't been able to talk very much lately due to my house and his increased practices. He wouldn't tell me why, but he had started doing one-on-one sessions with Porter and his coach.

"You should try to sleep on the plane," he advised. "We don't have plans tonight except to cuddle and watch movies, since I know you've said you haven't had much sleep lately."

"Thanks, Sam."

"Anything for you, babe."

The signs lit up to let us know we could get in line for boarding. "They're boarding us now. I'll see you in a few hours."

"Have a safe flight."

I hung up and headed to get in line. Once seated, I draped my blanket over my lap, put my sleep mask on, and curled up as comfortably as I could on an airplane seat.

Someone shook my shoulder, startling me awake. I pulled my sleep mask down and the flight attendant smile sympathetically at me. "Ma'am, we've landed. It's time to deboard."

I looked around and realized with a gasp that I was the last one onboard. "I'm so sorry!"

She pulled my suitcase down out of the overhead bin and

smiled. "It's alright. I hope you get a good night's rest tonight."

Quickly, I grabbed my backpack, slung it on, and hurried out of the airplane, my cheeks an inferno. I hated causing other people inconvenience.

Sam smiled when he saw me and asked, "Your nap was good?"

I scowled. "How did you know I napped?"

When I was close enough, he tugged on the sleep mask that was on top of my head. "Just a guess."

"Oh, my goodness," I gasped and quickly pulled it off and tried to finger brush my hair out.

He slipped his arms around my waist and pulled me in for a tight hug. "I missed you."

Resting my head against his chest, I drew in a deep breath of his cologne. "I missed you, too."

Leaning back, he kissed me deeply and I swayed a bit.

"Let's go pick up dinner and get you to my place," he said, linked our hand together, and grabbed my suitcase handle.

Three men carrying cameras rushed over snapping pictures and one asked, "Tucker, is this your girlfriend? The one you made the social media posts about?"

My eyes widened. Social media posts? What were they talking about?

"Excuse us, she just landed and needs to eat," Sam said and walked forward, his hand tightening around mine.

The men weren't detoured though. "What's your name? How long have you been dating?"

"Just ignore them," Sam whispered.

The men snapped several more pictures and I worried

what that could mean for Sam, but he didn't seem bothered by it.

"What social media posts are they talking about?"

Sam scowled down at me. "You mean you don't stalk me on social media like I stalk you?"

Now it was my turn to scowl. "I rarely go on there. My posts and pictures are mainly for my family that live out of state, so they can see what I'm up to."

He held the car door open for me and said, "Well, if you want to know what they're talking about, you'll have to look it up."

The brat knew I was an overly curious person. He also knew that I wouldn't do it while he was next to me.

He made me stay in the car while he ran in to pick up our dinner, so I used that time to check his social media.

My eyes immediately widened as I saw pictures of me and pictures of us on it. He also posted a few shirtless gym selfies with a pouty face and a comment about having to work out two states away from his girlfriend.

There were posts all the way back to when we'd met again at the skating rink in our hometown.

His recent posts were countdowns to him getting to see me again.

"It smells delicious," he boasted as he joined me in the car again.

Quickly, I put my phone away, not wanting him to catch me looking at his posts.

"Hopefully it tastes as good as it smells," I said.

It did taste as good as it smelled and I had to convince him to take it away from me so I didn't overeat.

Cuddled against his side, his warm, muscular arm around

me, I took a deep, cleansing breath. Being with him was so easy, so relaxing.

He trailed his fingertips up and down my arm, eyes focused on the movie, but still letting me know he was glad I was here.

"How late are your practices?" I asked. "Will we be able to eat dinner together?"

"I moved my sessions earlier so that I could make sure we were able to eat together," he said and looked down at me, smiling when he caught me staring at him. "See something you like, Mollie?"

I nodded. "I do."

His smile stuttered a bit, but he lowered his head and placed a chaste kiss on my lips. "Ditto."

"Are you alright, Sam? You seem ... off."

"Just tired, babe," he said and squeezed me tight. "Having you here makes it better."

"You sure there's nothing you want to talk about?" I asked.

He shook his head. "No, I'd rather just enjoy this time with you, soak up your presence while I have you here."

Getting up, I repositioned myself so that I sat straddling him, hands braced on the back of his couch on either side of his head. "Just sit with me?" I asked breathlessly. "Nothing else?"

His eyes widened, likely shocked at my assertive move. "Well, I suppose I could be convinced to do something else. What did you have in mind?"

"Well, it has been quite a while since I've seen my boyfriend and the last time we were together was ... explosive. Memorable. However, I realized that the last time we were together was about him showing me how he felt about me, and not me showing him that he deserves to be worshipped as well. That he is just as worthy as I am."

His hands stroked slowly up and down my back, causing my skin to break out in goosebumps. "Is that so?"

I nodded and kissed each of his cheeks, his forehead, his nose, and placed quick kisses across his jaw. "That's so."

His hands stilled, tightening on me as he let me kiss him. "And what did you have planned for this boyfriend?"

"I guess he'll just have to find out," I said and licked a line up his throat.

He groaned and gripped me a bit tighter. "Mm, that's one lucky boyfriend."

"Shh," I ordered. "No more talking."

"Yes, ma'am," he breathed.

I was tired, but dammit he'd unleashed something within me that opened a floodgate. One I worried would be hard to close once we separated again, but also not caring right now.

Pulling his shirt off, I stroked my fingertips down his muscles and said, "Such muscled perfection."

He opened his mouth, but I put my finger over his lips and said, "What did I say?"

He mimed zipping his lips and I smiled wide.

While this was about him, I knew I was going to enjoy it just as much.

"Now, onto the bed and strip those pants off. I've got fun to have."

CHAPTER 25

Sam

"I THINK WE NEED TO CONVINCE YOUR GIRLFRIEND TO move here," Coach teased. "You've never played better."

I panted and took a gulp of water before smiling at him. "If anyone could convince her, it would probably be you, Coach. You've got that silver tongue."

He patted my shoulder. "Your extra sessions are definitely paying off. Keep up the good work, Tucker."

"I'm going to beg her to come to our opening game," Porter said as he followed me to the locker room. "I bet you'll score ten goals if she's there."

"Opening night might be difficult for her to make," I said and rolled out my shoulders.

"Maybe I can bribe her with box seats for her and her friend, the one who likes me," he muttered to himself.

Laughing, I shook my head at him and said, "I appreciate it, but I'll be fine. She'll be at game three."

"Game three?" he asked. "That's against the Devils, right? That's a great game for her to be at, since they're likely our toughest competition this season."

"I'm off to the showers," I said as I shucked off my pads.

"Heading home to have dinner with your girl?" he asked.

I nodded. "She's making me curry."

"Lucky bastard," Martins muttered.

My phone beeped and I looked at it just in case it was important. My heart plummeted when I saw the message from Alicia.

> Alicia: Memorial Hospital. Hurry.

Tossing my towel back down, I rushed to grab my wallet and keys. My hands shook so hard that my keys jingled loudly.

"What's wrong?" Cap asked.

"Hospital," I said, unable to think beyond that. Mollie was hurt or injured or sick or something that had forced Alicia to take her to the hospital. I had to get there. I had to ...

"I'll drive," Cap said. "You're too panicked to be safe on the road."

I tossed him my keys as we both raced out of the rink and to my car. Cap thankfully drove fast, but it wasn't fast enough for me. My legs bounced nervously from the uncertainty. Couldn't Alicia have given me more than that?

As Cap and I ran inside the hospital towards the counter, Alicia waved at us from the emergency entrance.

"Where is she? What happened? Where?" I asked, spitting the questions out fast.

"She's in with the doctors in emergency," Alicia said.

"What happened?" Cap asked and rested his hand on her shoulder.

"Tiffany said something that pissed her off. I've never

seen Mollie mad, but she was livid. Tiffany punched Mollie and next thing I knew, they were beating the shit out of each other on the ice. Then Tiffany attacked her during a jumping practice and ... and ... her bone was sticking out, and ..." She ducked her head and Cap pulled her into his arms, rubbing her back.

"You'll need to wait out here," a guard said by the entrance. "I know she's your girl, but only family is allowed back."

"She doesn't have any family. I'm the closest she has," I told him and stepped forward to push by him.

Cap grabbed me and pulled me back. "Easy, Tuck. They'll let us talk to the doctor once she's stable. Let them do their jobs. Let's go wait in the waiting room."

The guard nodded at Cap. "I'll send the doctor out as soon as they're done."

I pushed Cap's arm away and spun around, stalking towards the waiting room. I couldn't sit, though; my heart felt like it was in my throat and I was about to puke it right up.

Holy shit. Tiffany had attacked her? What? Over me? That was ridiculous. Why had Tiffany done that? What was wrong with her? A broken leg? That was going to seriously hinder her progress. She was going to be devastated.

Cap talked softly with Alicia, comforting her. I knew they'd dated before and were still friends.

Brit burst into the waiting room, eyes frantic. "Where is she?"

"Still inside," Alicia whispered.

Her eyes darkened and she asked, "Where's Tiffany?" Her hands balled into fists and she stomped over to Alicia. "Where is that stupid bitch?"

"She's in the back, too," Alicia answered.

"I'm going to rip her fucking head off," Brit snapped.

"Whoa, what's going on?" Cap asked and grabbed her arm, keeping her from going to the ER section.

"Tiffany provoked and attacked her. Jessica called me and told me what happened since she was there, too. Tiffany taunted Mollie, talking about ..." Her eyes darted to me. "... things. Mollie told her to shut up, that she was jealous a country bumpkin like her had Tucker's attention, and Tiffany and she got in a fight, but it was broken up. Then later, during a jump practice, Tiffany attacked Mollie, making her fall and break her leg."

"I haven't been with Tiff in over a year! And it was only a one-night stand!" I snapped. I gripped my hair and sat hard on one of the chairs.

"It's not your fault," Cap said. "We all know Tiff is a psycho. That's why I warned you away from her. I didn't think she was capable of something like this, though."

"It didn't help that Mollie's surpassed her in camp," Alicia said and sniffled. "Mollie's been doing so well and it upset some of the girls. They thought she was a novice, but she's clearly been working extra hard the past three weeks because she did moves I never expected someone as new as her to do." Alicia looked at me and said, "I'm sorry, Sam. I should have protected her better. I should have—"

I shook my head and said, "You're not at fault. I shouldn't ... I shouldn't have got her involved here. I should have ..."

I should have let her go the last time we saw each other. I should have ended things then, like Cap said.

"Tucker," the doctor called.

I jumped out of my chair and rushed over to him, the others right on my heels.

He was a doctor we'd all seen multiple times after scuffles and when friends got injured, so he thankfully knew who we were.

"How is she?" I asked, throat tight and worry making my entire body shake. "How is Mollie?"

"She's stable. She had to have emergency surgery and it was successful. She's unconscious still." He looked at our group and said, "I can let only one of you back. When she's awake and we check her concussion—"

"Concussion on top of her leg?" Alicia asked and gasped, her hands going up to her mouth.

He nodded. "She's definitely suffered head trauma. From the attacker's testimony, she slammed her head into the ice multiple times when they fought, before the jump incident."

"Tiffany's awake!" Brit shouted and started to walk towards the door, but Cap grabbed her around the waist, picking her up so she couldn't go.

"The cops are speaking to her now." He nodded at Alicia. "They're going to want to talk to you as well."

"Can I see her?" I asked. "Please."

"As long as you're sure you can control yourself," he said sternly.

I nodded.

He looked at Cap. "You going to wait here?"

Cap nodded. "I'll stay with the girls out here. Keep 'em in hand."

Doc nodded and headed back towards the ER. "Come on, Tucker. I'll take you to her room."

117

CHAPTER 26

Mollie

My entire body felt abnormally heavy. Like I was underwater, or like I had a dozen blankets piled on top of me.

There was strange beeping and weird smells as well.

I could breathe, so that was a good sign.

My eyes felt too heavy and wouldn't open, though.

"Mm," I groaned.

"Mollie?" Sam asked, his voice sounded far away. "Don't move!" he ordered me. "Doc! Doc! She's waking up."

Doc?

Oh, right. The fight with Tiffany and her attack. The beeping made sense now. I was in a hospital.

My eyes finally started to open, but the lights were so bright, I quickly closed them again.

Someone's hands touched me and an unfamiliar male voice asked, "Can you open your eyes for me?"

I blinked them open, able to since the doctor was blocking the lights a bit.

He smiled and shined a light into my eyes. "Do you remember your name?"

"M-Mollie," I answered and immediately winced. My throat hurt and it felt super tight.

He nodded. "Good. And do you know why you're here?"

"F-F-Fight," I answered. God, why did my throat hurt so much?

"Good," he said and nodded. "Your throat will feel better after some water. You had to have emergency surgery on your leg."

Oh! That was right.

"Your leg is in a cast and you do have bruising and a concussion, which is why you have a headache."

Ah, that explained it.

"Don't move too fast or it may make you dizzy and nauseous," he ordered me. He turned to someone in the room and said, "Don't ask her to talk until she's finished a cup of water, *slowly*."

"Understood," Sam said.

The doctor left and Sam sat next to me, smiling warmly. His hair was tousled and some stuck to his face from sweat and he had bags under his eyes. "Hello, beautiful."

I tried to raise my hand to touch his hair, but he caught my hand as I tried to lift it and set it back on the bed.

"Don't move. You've been here a few days. The doctors have taken great care of you. I was getting worried when you didn't wake up for so long."

Had he been here the whole time? That would explain his rumpled appearance. Looking at his outfit, I realized he was in the tank top and compression shorts he wore under his gear. He must have raced here from practice without changing. How long ago was that?

I squeezed his hand and tried to swallow, but it hurt. He

must have noticed my cringe because he grabbed a cup of water from the table that had a straw and held it up for me.

"Slow, small sips. Don't rush it."

Despite wanting to chug it, I took a small sip like he had said to.

"I already called Marie and I just texted her while the doc was checking you out."

It was like he could read my mind.

He dropped his head down and rested it on our joined hands. "I'm so glad you're okay. When ... when I saw Alicia's text and heard what happened ..."

I stroked my thumb over his fingers since that was all I could really do.

After a moment, I realized that he had fallen asleep.

A nurse came in a bit later, checked me over, and asked how my pain was. She gave me more pain medication and some more water and smiled softly at Sam.

"He's been at your side all week. Refused to leave you and even ignored Porter's threats. He really cares about you."

All week? How long had I been here?

"Slowly and carefully drinking the water will help your throat. And keep resting."

She looked at Sam one more time before turning and leaving.

Sam's phone pinged, but he didn't stir. It was on the chair on the side of the room, so there was no way for me to get it.

With a sigh, I closed my eyes and relaxed on the bed again, happy to be holding his hand while he slept.

Feeling safe with him at my side, knowing he would protect me if anyone came into the room.

So grateful that the doctors took care of me.

Yet, even after however long I'd been asleep, I was still tired.

CHAPTER 27

Sam

MOLLIE ENDED UP STAYING IN THE HOSPITAL FOR another four days and when we were able to leave, I forced her to let me push her in a wheelchair.

The cops had come to talk to her, but their questions were simple, just needing her statement because they already had testimony from everyone else who had been there, and the video surveillance.

Tiffany was going to be charged for attacking Mollie, but she was currently free. Thankfully, she was smart enough to leave campus and go back home for awhile. Rumor around campus was that her parents were pissed and considering transferring her to a different college.

I, for one, was one hundred percent in favor of that idea. I wasn't sure how I would react if I saw her.

Mollie could have flown home, but the truth was, I didn't want to let her go. The camp had been cancelled due to the attack and she was past the date she was supposed to return home.

I didn't want her to go. And yet, I also felt that this was

my fault. She wouldn't have been hurt if she hadn't been involved with me.

The news had spread far and wide. The articles were so sensationalized: *Hockey player's girlfriend attacked by rival love interest.*

Absolute trash.

I made a statement, one that the team's legal group reviewed and edited several times. Ultimately, I had still added a bit of my own words to it against their advice, but I didn't care.

This had nothing to do with hockey.

This had to do with a woman attacking another woman unprovoked, out of jealousy. Over a man that was never hers to begin with.

It still made my blood boil and I hated that I hadn't been there to protect her.

"Brit asked if you'd be okay with her and Cap coming over later," I said softly as I set her on her feet so I could unlock the door.

"Okay," she replied, but she didn't seem enthusiastic about it.

"I can tell them you're not ready for visitors yet. Brit's been really worried about you, though, and hasn't stopped asking to come see you." She'd come a few times while Mollie had been asleep, but seeing her with the cast on her leg and face severely bruised had been too hard for her.

I understood. It had been hard for me as well.

Marie had asked for pictures, but I absolutely refused. I video called her once so she could talk to Mollie, but both had just ended up crying so we'd had to end the call pretty early.

"I shouldn't be, but I'm tired," she whispered.

"The doctor said that you might be tired for a bit longer. You don't need to worry about it and can rest as long as you want or need to."

"You need ... practice."

I had missed a lot of practice, but Cap had talked things over with Coach and they assured me it was fine since we were still in off-season, but made me promise to at least workout.

When Mollie was sleeping, I did mini workouts that consisted of pushups, sit ups, squats, planks, and burpees. It felt good to work out and gave me something to do while she was sleeping.

"I don't want you to lose your edge because you are taking care of me or get in trouble with your coach. I have crutches that I can use and—"

"I got permission to skip practice as long as I'm focusing on my workouts, which I do while you sleep. You don't need to worry about anything, Mollie. Just focus on getting better."

After I got her situated on the coach, controller in her hand so she could find a movie to watch, I started making lunch for us.

The food at the hospital hadn't been awful, but it hadn't been great, either. We both needed some good food.

Thankfully, Brit had wanted to be useful, so she'd done some shopping for us, filling up the fridge.

"Is chicken and rice okay for lunch?" I asked.

"Yeah," she replied weakly.

She started the movie while I made the food. When I brought our bowls over, I realized she was watching a hockey movie.

"What's this?" I asked.

"I wanted to learn a bit more about hockey since I don't know that much," she explained. Smiling up at me she said, "You know, since I'm dating a hockey player."

My smile was a bit forced, but she didn't seem to notice. Seeing her so injured made me want to keep her by my side and protect her, but it made another part of me seriously consider breaking things off so that something like this wouldn't happen again in the future.

"You know what happened isn't your fault, right?" she asked me softly and set a hand on my arm.

"You a mind reader?" I teased.

She smiled and said, "No, but I know what I would be thinking if I were in your shoes. Tiffany was just a crazy, jealous bitch. If it hadn't been me, it would have been whoever else you dated. Or, perhaps it was me because she hated that I was a country bumpkin and still had your attention. Plus, I was kicking her butt in the skating camp. Anyway, none of this is your fault. I would have come to the camp even if we weren't dating right now. If you had broken up with me before, I just would have fought her harder thinking she was sleeping with you."

"You're the only one for me," I whispered.

CHAPTER 28

Mollie

"You're the only one for me," Sam whispered as he scooped some food out of his bowl.

My eyes felt like they were going to pop out of my head and my mouth dropped open in surprise.

He frowned a moment, eyes widened as if in surprise, then nodded and turned to me. "I've been doing a lot of thinking, like *a lot*, and the one thing I know for certain is that I don't want to lose you. You are the lightning on a rainy night, the spark that keeps me going even in dark times. Ask Cap and Coach, while you were here, I was playing better than ever before. I know there is a lot for us to figure out, a lot of things that need to be decided for our future and now isn't the right moment for that. However, I know without a doubt that I don't want a future that doesn't involve you, Mollie."

Tears welled up in my eyes as I stared at him and felt the conviction with which he said the words I had always wanted to hear directed at me.

"Promise me that you won't ice me out? Promise me that you will work with me to secure a future where we're together?" He took both of my hands in his and gently kissed my knuckles.

This man was quite possibly the most perfect man I could have ever met and I knew I was crazy lucky to have him by my side.

I nodded and sniffled. "I promise."

He kissed me deeply, but his hold on me was gentle since I was still in a leg cast.

"And promise you won't give up on ice skating?" he asked.

Laughing softly and shaking my head, I said, "Alicia and some of the other girls from the camp have been messaging me daily, sending me examples of others coming back from injuries similar to mine. Don't worry, I'm going to focus on my rehab and try my hardest to get back out on the ice. It wasn't like I was on the Olympic team before this anyway, so as long as I can do it and enjoy it, that's all I care about."

Honestly, the attack made me even more determined to get back to it. I was going to prove that I could skate and while I knew I wasn't going to the Olympics or anything crazy like that, I was determined to win at least a couple small competitions.

"Have you found a rehabilitation center?" he asked and released me so we could eat.

I sighed. "There aren't any close to our town. I'm still looking."

"Alicia said there's one just two blocks from the stadium," he commented.

"Sam, you know I can't stay here. I have to get back to my job. I'm already late." Thankfully, the Director had stepped in and assured me I could take my time. Taking my time didn't mean staying here for months, though. The doctor I'd talked to at the hospital had said my rehabilitation was going to be several months and that I likely shouldn't skate for at least six months.

Six months was a long time when I was itching to get back out there again already. However, I knew it was better to wait until I was fully recovered, and I knew I definitely wasn't doing anything while in a cast. Thankfully, it had been a clean break and they felt confident that I would be able to resume my previous level of activity.

"This rehab center is one of the best. All the athletes here use them. There aren't very many rehab centers within a fifty-mile radius of our hometown, especially good ones. You could stay with me and go to the center and—"

I heard what he was saying, but I couldn't just leave my life.

Could I?

CHAPTER 29

Mollie

It was important to start my rehabilitation as soon as possible. And it was important to go to a good one. And I knew there weren't many near me at home, but ...

"I don't know," I said, interrupting Sam. "Let me think about it."

He nodded and turned back to watch the movie. "Take however long you need."

Halfway through the movie, Brit and Porter showed up.

After quick hellos, they sat down to watch the movie with us, suddenly engrossed.

Sam smiled down at me and kissed the top of my head. "Your pain okay? Time for a pill?"

I nodded. "Time for a pill."

He hurried to the kitchen to get me a fresh glass of water and a pain pill, which I quickly took and resettled against his side.

When the movie ended, Brit, Sam, and Porter argued over some of the aspects of the movie and I enjoyed hearing their takes on it.

It was nice to be here ... with them.

While I did love my job, I really did want to move forward with ice skating. And, I really did want to continue this relationship. Sam had really shown his intentions and it felt like it was my turn as well.

"What are you scowling about over there?" Brit asked, sitting down carefully next to me while Sam and Porter went to the kitchen to grab more drinks and snacks.

I watched Sam head to the bathroom before answering.

"Debating accepting Sam's invitation to stay here for a few months for rehab," I admitted.

Her eyes widened and she smiled. "That would be awesome! We could hang out and I know the team would love you to stay."

"Stay?" Porter asked as he rejoined us, setting the items from his arms on the coffee table.

"Sam has very generously offered to let me stay here to go to the rehab center down the street," I explained. "I'm considering it."

Porter's eyes widened. "You totally should! I'll even pay for your rehab!"

My mouth dropped. "What? Why would you pay for it?"

"If you're here, Tucker will play better. If Tucker plays better, the team benefits, especially me. I'm loaded, thanks to my parents, which I'm sure you noticed from the mansion I live in. Paying for your rehab is a drop in the bucket for me, and if it is going to benefit the team like I know it will, it's worth it. More than worth it."

"I don't know about all that," I said, and laughed nervously. "I doubt I'm as much of a benefit as you say."

"You are," Porter said with certainty.

"Just think about it," Brit urged. "It will make me feel better to be able to see you each day and know you're close by, healing and getting better."

"Like I said, I'm still thinking," I said quickly.

"Well, if there's anything I can do to help convince you, say the word," Porter said seriously. "You want box seats for your friend and you at the games? Done. You want signed merch from every single one of the members? Done. You want a swimsuit calendar of me, signed, for your friend? Done."

My head fell back as I laughed. "She would definitely appreciate that."

"Oh, he's got a stack at the house," Brit said.

My eyes widened. "What?" He'd been serious?

"He did a swimsuit calendar shoot as a fundraiser for the team. Brought in thousands of dollars," she explained and nodded.

"Okay, I definitely need one of those," I said.

"Done," Porter agreed.

"What's done?" Sam asked.

"I'm giving her an autographed copy of my swimsuit calendar."

Sam froze and his eyes narrowed. "What?"

"For Marie," I said and laughed at the jealousy practically radiating off of him.

CHAPTER 30

Sam

OF COURSE THE CALENDAR WAS FOR MARIE AND NOT Mollie. I was an idiot.

However, I loved the laugh that my outrage had caused Mollie. It was the first laugh I'd heard from her since the accident.

Taking my seat again next to Mollie, I kissed the side of her head and smiled at the contented sigh she released as she relaxed against me. She probably didn't even realize she'd made it.

Brit and Porter whispered conspiratorially while I chose another hockey movie for us to watch. It was clear that Mollie liked our debating afterwards, if the smirk on her face was anything to go by.

This was what I'd always wanted. Someone at my side who I could be myself with. Someone I could *relax* with.

Mollie wasn't like the girls trying to tie me down or trying to get pregnant to tie me down. She didn't care that I was a hockey player. She didn't care if I joined the NHL or not.

She cared about me. If I quit hockey and wanted to

return to our town to be a paper delivery boy, she'd be fine with it. If I wanted to start a business, she'd be fine with it. All she cared about was me.

It was … freeing.

"Hey, when's the Autumn Festival again?" I asked her.

"First weekend in August," she answered and tilted her head to look up at me. "Why?"

"Well, I was thinking, if you did decide to stay here, which I'm not pressuring you. But, if you did decide to stay here, we could go back to the town that weekend, pick up some more clothes and things you'd need, and visit Marie and my mama at the same time. Plus, we could convince Cap here to go with us and wouldn't that be an even greater gift to Marie? Might make it easier to break the news that you're going to be staying with me for a few months, too."

Her eyes widened and she looked at Porter.

"I've always wanted to see the town you grew up in and meet your mom," Porter agreed with a nod.

"Can I come, too?" Brit asked hopefully.

"Of course you could," Mollie said with a soft laugh. "Though, you'll probably find our small town boring."

"We should look for a hotel," Brit said and pulled her phone out.

"Nonsense," Mollie said immediately. "You're welcome to stay in my home. It's still a work in progress, but the rooms are nice."

"Oh!" I said and smiled down at her. "You're going to let me see your new home?"

She blushed a bit and said, "It's nothing special."

"It's yours, so it's special," I whispered and stroked my thumb across her reddened cheek.

"Won't you have practices?" she asked quickly.

"Not over the weekend," Porter answered. "Plus, I'm not passing up an opportunity to see where you two came from. See where the magic started."

Mollie's cheeks reddened again and I kissed one of them.

"Always blushing," I teased.

"Tickets are pricey," she whispered.

"We're saving on our hotel costs thanks to you," Porter reminded her. "Plus, it would be nice to get away from the craziness of the city for a bit."

She laughed and shook her head. "Oh, you won't get away from craziness. It's just a different flavor."

"Variety is the spice of life," Porter said with a wide smile. "I will enjoy seeing the craziness. It's settled. We're going. I'll book the tickets."

"But I haven't even confirmed if I'm staying," Mollie countered.

"You know my offer is too good to pass up. I'll even throw in an ereader filled with as many books as you want," Porter said, and pointed at her. "Just accept it so Tucker can stop pouting all the damn time."

Mollie sucked in a breath at the book offer.

My eyes widened. Wait, had they been talking about her staying?

Mollie laughed. "You really are something, Porter."

He winked. "You don't know the half of it."

"Don't flirt with my girl," I snapped at the same time Brit smacked his arm.

That just made him laugh as he resumed looking at his phone.

"Fine," Mollie said after a few seconds of quiet. "But I

want everything you promised me, plus you coming to meet Marie at the Autumn Festival."

Porter walked over and held out his hand. "Deal."

"Wait," I said, and grabbed Mollie's hand before she could shake his. "What deal did you two make while I was in the bathroom?"

"Don't you fret, Tuck. I've got it all worked out and we're going to win the championship for sure now." Porter knocked my hand away and shook hands with Mollie. "I look forward to seeing you in the box every game."

My eyes widened again and I looked down at her. "What?"

She smiled and asked, "Can I add one more request?"

Porter scowled. "What else could you want?"

"Well, since I'm Tucker's girlfriend, don't I need a jersey to wear to the games?"

Before Porter could answer, I grabbed her face between my hands and kissed her. She wanted to wear my jersey! It was such a simple gesture, one the puck bunnies made all the time, but coming from her, it made my heart flutter like a schoolgirl.

"You won't regret this," I whispered.

She laughed and said, "Don't count your ducks before they hatch, Sam."

CHAPTER 31

Sam

"THAT WAS YOUR BEST PLAYING YET," COACH PRAISED me and patted my shoulder. "Keep that up, son and you'll be recruited before the championship game."

"Thanks, Coach," I said, preening a little at the praise.

He looked up at the stands where Mollie sat reading from the ereader that Porter had purchased her, as promised, and filled with books. She, Brit, and a few other girls had started their own book club and they were reading some fantasy book that people kept calling "spicy." Whatever that meant.

"Normally, I tell players to stay away from girls during the season, but this is the exception." Coach patted my shoulder as he walked away. "You better keep her happy."

"Yes, sir. That's the goal," I replied.

She looked up, noticed me looking, and smiled at me. I blew her a kiss and she ducked her head down.

I didn't think I would ever get tired of her adorable shyness.

After showering and changing, I hurried to meet Mollie

at the entrance. We had a tight schedule and I didn't want to keep her waiting.

I stopped at the corner when I heard her speaking to someone, peeking around, I saw her on the phone, sitting in her wheelchair, anxiously tugging on her shirt collar.

"What do you mean? I don't understand. You said I could come back once I was ready. Why are you changing ... You know I love my job. You know I ... Even if I came back today, I'm in a wheelchair and ... This isn't fair, Director. I've spent the last two years doing everything I could for the library. I worked overtime and weekends without getting paid and created programs for the children and ... I can't make my leg heal faster!"

Walking quickly to her, I dropped to a squat so I could look in her eyes without her being forced to tilt her head back.

"What's wrong?" I asked softly.

Tears dripped down her face and she shook her head at me. "Yes, I understand what you're saying, Director. I ..." She looked down at her phone and sobbed, letting it drop into her lap. "She fired me. After all I've done."

"She can't fire you because you're injured and in a wheelchair. That's illegal," I said immediately, anger rising in my chest.

"She's firing me because I requested a two-month break. She said that she needs to find a replacement and that we both know they can't accommodate someone with a serious leg injury, but that's bullshit!" Covering her face with her hands, she cried harder, her back shaking with her sobs.

I wrapped my arms around her and pet her hair. "I'm so sorry, Mollie."

"I love that job. Wh-What am I going to do now? I just bought my house and had enough savings to cover two months, but I can't afford longer than that. What am I going to do?"

"Tucker, Mollie, we need to leave!" Porter called as he opened the door. When he saw our position, his smile turned into a scowl. "What's wrong? Is it her pain? Did it get worse?"

Mollie wiped her face and sniffed loudly twice. "Let's go. We can't miss our flight."

"We'll figure something out," I promised her. "Don't worry."

She nodded, but I saw her lip tremble. She was trying so hard to stuff her pain down. I hated it, but we did need to leave.

As I pushed her wheelchair out the door Porter held open for us, I whispered to Porter, "Later."

He frowned harder, but nodded in acknowledgement.

Once inside the SUV, seated next to Brit, she smiled and joked with Brit as though nothing had happened.

I put her wheelchair in the back, next to the suitcases. We'd packed and put our suitcases in the car before practice so we could leave right after.

Porter looked back at her, then at me, as we buckled our belts in the front seats. He picked up on her desire to not discuss it and cheerfully smiled at them and asked, "Are you ready?"

"Yes!" Brit cheered. "I could barely sleep last night."

Mollie laughed and said, "I think you're hyping this up too much. You're going to be sorely disappointed when you realize that it's not great."

Porter drove away from the stadium and onto the freeway, headed to the airport.

"Oh, hush. We're going to have a ton of fun," Brit argued and rested her head on Mollie's shoulder. "I heard Tuck's mom is going to make us cookies."

"She's been baking for two days," I replied. "Cookies, brownies, and is even making us dinner when we arrive."

"I haven't had a motherly home cooked meal in years," Brit said and said happily. "I can't wait."

"Don't worry, you'll get lots of homecooked meals this weekend," Mollie promised. "And a lot of attention from everyone in the town."

"Porter is used to being the center of attention. He thrives off of it," Brit teased.

"You learn to accept it when you're this good looking," Porter said, smiling wide.

I relaxed into my seat and said, "Well, at least it will keep the attention off of me this time. That way I can actually take Mollie on a proper date."

She scoffed. "Like the women are going to stop hitting on you just because Porter is there. Besides, this weekend is a group trip, not one for us to go on a date."

"We have to make sure to keep up on our reading so the others don't read ahead and spoil something for us," Brit said. "I'm only on chapter ten."

"Oh, I'm ahead of you already," Mollie said and laughed. "You're getting to a good part."

"No spoilers!" Brit shouted and they both laughed.

It hurt to know that Mollie had lost her job because I'd gotten involved in her life. I had to find a way to help her. A way to make things right. Maybe if I went and talked to the library Director, I could convince her to let Mollie return in two months.

Not that I wanted her to go back in two months, but I knew I had to be happy with what time I got with her.

There had to be something I could do for her. Some way to help her when it felt like all I had done so far was cause her issues.

I was going to try my hardest to make things right, to make her happy. Even if it meant getting a lawyer involved or crawling on my knees to the Director.

CHAPTER 32
Mollie

By the time we landed, my leg was killing me. Nothing I did on the plane had helped and even my pain meds weren't working as well. Sam had tried to distract me, but nothing worked.

We drove through our small town and Brit kept gasping in delight, a huge smile on her face.

It *was* a cute town, full of charm, but now my feelings were marred by the Director's call. It hurt, but I wasn't going to let my plight ruin the trip for Porter and Brit. They deserved to have a great time still, especially since Porter had paid for everything.

Brit gasped loudly as we pulled up to my house. "This is your house? Oh, my goodness! It's so cute."

"Thanks," I replied and smiled up at the Victorian. It was cute, even if slightly run down.

Sam got my wheelchair out, opened my door, picked me up, and set me in it. I had complained the first time, but he swore I was light and so I stopped complaining.

As he pushed me up the path to the front door, the door opened and Marie ran out wearing a cute sundress with her hair curled. She threw her arms around me and squealed.

I laughed as I hugged her back. "Well, hello. It's obvious you didn't miss me one bit."

She pushed back and tweaked my nose. "I missed you more than sweet tea in the summer." Standing up, she hugged Sam. "Hello, Sam. Thanks for taking care of her for me."

He seemed shocked by the hug, but patted her back before saying, "You don't have to thank me for that."

When they stepped back, she realized we weren't alone and her eyes widened.

"Marie, I'd like you to meet Brit and Jackson Porter. This is my best friend Marie."

She smoothed her dress down and smiled. "It's nice to meet you." She held out her hand and shook first with Brit and then Porter.

I rolled my eyes at the obvious attempt to not come off as a fan girl when she clearly was.

"It's nice to finally meet you, Marie," Porter said and smiled warmly. "I've heard you are a Ravens fan."

She nodded. "I don't miss a game on TV."

"Thank you. That makes me so happy to hear," he said.

Her cheeks reddened a bit. "Well, let's not stand out here and let the bugs get us. I've got the rooms made up for you all. Mol, I set you up in one of the downstairs rooms for now."

"You're the best," I praised.

She winked at me. "Don't you forget it." Spinning on her heel, she walked inside and Sam pushed me in behind her. "I also did some shopping so your pantry and fridge are stocked."

"We really appreciate your help," Sam said. He pushed me into the living room, picked me up, and set me on the couch.

I sighed in relief at finally being able to stretch out. Without asking, Sam filled a glass of water and brought me a pain pill.

"Thank you," I whispered as I took it.

"I know the flight wasn't easy for you," he whispered as he pet my hair. "Hopefully, you'll be better after some rest here."

"I will be," I said confidently. "We have to leave in about thirty minutes to meet your mom, right?"

He nodded.

"You just relax and let me give them the tour of your adorable house," Marie said. "Come on, we'll start on the second floor."

I watched them all traipse up the stairs, Marie and Brit chatting about the house, and felt both joy and sadness simultaneously. What was I going to do about work? About the house?

I loved this house, but ... maybe it would be better to sell it. I had made enough improvements that it should sell for more than what I had paid. I could hire someone to make a few more improvements to really help it sell.

Thinking about it made me even more exhausted. I closed my eyes and sighed.

"What's that big sigh about?" Marie asked as she sat next to me.

I opened my eyes and watched Brit, Porter, and Sam walk around the living room, whispering about something.

"I forgot I haven't had a chance to tell you the latest," I said.

Marie's eyes widened. "What?"

"I got fired today."

CHAPTER 33

Mollie

MARIE STOOD WITH HER HANDS CLENCHED INTO FISTS. "What? The Director fired you? On what grounds?"

"She said they can't be without someone for two months and there's not much I can do while in a wheelchair."

Her mouth dropped. "She did *not* say that?"

I nodded.

"That's illegal! Is she stupid? Wait, don't answer that, we know she's not the sharpest tool in the shed. I cannot believe she would do this to you after everything you've done. No. No way. I'm not going to let her get away with this. I'm callin' Mrs. Abernathy."

Mrs. Abernathy was one of the women from the founding families, a force to be reckoned with when she was angry, and she could definitely be one to change the Director's mind if anyone could.

"You don't have to do that," I said quickly. "I was thinking I might just sell this place and—"

"You hush up, right now!" Marie said and pulled out her phone. "She thinks she can get away with this just because it's a small town? Hah. She won't get away with this *because* we're a small town. I am going to set the gossipers on fire right now." She held the phone up to her ear and when someone answered, she got the sweetest smile on her face and said, "Hello, Mrs. Abernathy. Did those strawberries I gave you yesterday pair well with that tea? Oh, I'm so glad. Oh, well I have another reason for calling you." She walked out of the room and I cringed.

Part of me was glad for her help, but I knew it wasn't going to endear me to the Director. It might affect my work environment negatively.

"What's going on?" Porter asked with a scowl as he turned to me.

"She's on a warpath," I said. "I think it might be better to just accept my defeat and sell this place."

His eyes widened and he sat on the coffee table in front of me so he could look at me easier. "Tell me what's going on? I noticed that you were upset before we left the arena."

I repeated what had happened to Porter and he rolled his eyes. "That's a one-way ticket to a wrongful termination case. I can definitely help you with that. My uncle is a lawyer and he owes me a favor."

"I don't want to piss off the Director," I said quickly.

"You know you can move in with me," Sam said quickly. "Not that I want you to lose this nice house, but ..." He shrugged.

"I'm going to get that bitch fired," Marie said as she came back into the living room. "No one goes after my best friend. Mrs. Abernathy was livid when she heard what happened."

I covered my face with my hands and whispered, "I'm not going to be able to show my face around town."

"You didn't do anything wrong," Sam said.

"She should be the one hiding, not you," Porter agreed.

"Exactly!" Brit said.

"Let's talk about it later. We're supposed to head to Sam's house for dinner," I said and looked at Marie. "Can you help me change?"

She smirked. "Don't want to wear your airplane clothes to meet his mom?"

"You already know my mom," Sam countered. "She changed your diapers several times and babysat you when we were in elementary school."

"Oh my god, that is adorable," Brit gasped. "I didn't know that."

Marie nodded. "Sam's ma helped take care of Mollie after her dad left and her mom, well, her mom worsened."

Porter looked at me. "I thought you had a standard small town childhood?"

Marie laughed humorlessly. "She got the alcoholic parent version, but thankfully our town helped out so that she didn't suffer too much. My parents basically adopted her when we became best friends in fifth grade."

"Yes, I had some not so fun times, but they were overshadowed by my friends and the others in this town." I had forgotten that I'd spent a lot of time as a child playing with Sam at his house. "Now, Marie, help me change so we can go. I am not going over to see Mrs. Tucker smelling of sweat when it's my first time officially going over as her son's girlfriend."

"Whatever makes you happy," Marie conceded. "Sam, carry your girl to the room over here. I'll help her change."

"Thank you."

Brit followed and said, "I'll help with your makeup."

"Good idea, she needs all the help she can get in that area," Marie agreed.

"Hey!" I shouted, but both just laughed and followed Sam as he carried me.

CHAPTER 34
Sam

MOLLIE LOOKED GORGEOUS WHEN I WAS FINALLY LET back in her room to get her to go to my mom's.

"Maybe we could just stay home," I whispered in her ear as I picked her up and carried her towards the door.

She blushed and turned her head down. "Stop it."

"You two are adorable," Marie squealed. "I can't wait to see what your babies look like."

"Oh my god, Marie!" Mollie snapped. "Shut up!"

Brit snickered from the living room where she and Porter waited for us.

While I didn't want kids anytime soon, I bet our kids *would* be super adorable. The cutest babies ever.

"Do you need anything else?" I asked as we headed past the kitchen.

"The wine!" she shouted, throwing her arm back to point behind us.

"I got it," Brit said, and grabbed the bottle of wine from the counter.

"You lot have fun. I'm going home to binge the new

season of my favorite show. Call me if you need anything, otherwise, I will see you all tomorrow at the festival." She patted Mollie on the head as she skipped by and out the front door.

"She's quite the character," Porter commented.

Mollie chuckled. "You don't know the half of it. Wait until you see her tomorrow."

The drive to Mom's was quick and, unsurprisingly, she waited for us out front when we arrived.

"My baby!" she shouted as I got out of the car. Wrapping me in a tight hug and rocking us back and forth.

I kissed the top of her head. "Hi, Mama. Miss me?"

She tweaked my earlobe. "You know it." Looking past me, she smiled at Brit. "Hello, you must be Brit."

"Yes, ma'am. It's nice to meet you," Brit said and shook hands with Mom, who quickly pulled her into a hug.

"We're huggers here, darlin'. Handshakes are for business partners, not friends or family."

I went to go grab Mollie, but Porter had already picked her up. They were whispering with serious expressions on their faces and Mollie's cheeks were slightly red.

What were they talking about?

"Mollie!" Mom yelled and rushed over to gently set her hand on the cast on her leg. "I heard all about the terrible accident. You poor thing. You've always had the worst luck of anyone I've met, 'cept that old hound with three legs we used to have."

"I'm fine, Mrs. Tucker," she said quickly.

"Sam been takin' care of you? If not, you let me know and I'll set him straight," Mom said seriously.

"He's been great," Mollie said with a soft smile. Her eyes

darted to me before returning to Mom. "More than hospitable."

"It's nice to meet you, Mrs. Tucker," Porter said. "I'd hug you, but my arms are a bit full." He raised Mollie a bit higher, making her blush return.

Mom hugged them both. "Carry my future daughter-in-law inside, will you? Let's get out of this heat and away from these bugs. I swear, they triple in population right before the Autumn Festival every year."

Once inside, Porter set Mollie on the couch and I pulled him back a bit. "What were you two talkin' about?"

"Tuck, you've got to take a breath. You know I'm not after your girl," he said sternly.

"I'm not worried about that," I said quickly. "You two looked super serious, so I wanted to know what you said to her."

Mom sat in her reclining chair and her face turned serious. Instead of probing Porter more, I turned to face them. Things rarely went well when she got that expression.

"I heard about what Tanya Smith did. Don't you fret one bit. We won't let this stand. No one in this town is going to be treated so unfairly, especially not you. You've dealt with more than your fair share of BS for ten lifetimes."

Mollie's eyes watered a bit. "Maybe it's for the best," she whispered.

"Child, that's nonsense and you know it. That old spinster is just mad you snagged a handsome man like Samuel, despite being a wallflower, while she's been pursuing every man in the tri county area without a match."

"Ma!" I shouted.

Mollie's cheeks turned red and Brit and Porter were trying, and failing, to hide their smiles.

She waved her hand dismissively at me before facing Mollie again. "Don't let her ruin your time here and don't you worry about your job. We'll get things handled and you can decide what you want to do later. There's no rush, and you need to focus solely on resting and healing. Nothing else matters. We'll have your house taken care of while you're gone, too. Now, everyone to the kitchen so we can eat!"

Mollie covered her face with her hands and took a few shuddering breaths.

Porter and Brit headed to the kitchen with Mom, giving us a bit of privacy.

"You okay?" I asked and set a hand on her thigh, above her cast.

"No."

"Pain?" I asked, concerned that she had already developed a tolerance to her medicine.

"Embarrassment," she admitted.

Laughing, I gently grabbed her wrists and pulled them down so I could see her face. "Because she called you a wallflower?"

She nodded and avoided looking in my eyes.

"You are the prettiest wallflower in the tri county area," I whispered and kissed her cheek.

"Sam!" she gasped and glared at me. "Rude."

Laughing, I picked her up and carried her to the kitchen, setting her in the chair beside Mom. "Just speaking the truth, babe."

"Insufferable," she muttered.

And she loved every minute of it.

After eating enough to make my jeans fit too snug and accepting leftovers, we returned to Mollie's house. Everyone was exhausted, jet lagged and decided to go to sleep even though it was barely nine o'clock.

Mollie lay across my chest, her fingers stroking my shoulder as she drifted slowly to sleep.

For the first time in a month, I fell asleep with a smile on my face.

CHAPTER 35

Sam

AGAINST MY WISHES, MY BODY WOKE ME UP AT FIVE a.m., so I took the opportunity to go out for a quick jog.

To my surprise, Porter was putting his shoes on when I headed towards the door.

"Care if I join you?" I asked.

He smiled. "I'd appreciate it, since I might otherwise get lost."

Laughing, I shook my head. "It's pretty impossible to get lost in a town this small."

After a quick stretch and grabbing water, we headed out at a nice, slow jog.

"Sleep well?" I asked.

He nodded. "The bed is really comfortable. I don't usually sleep well in unfamiliar places, but this house feels ..."

"Warm?" I offered.

He nodded again. "Exactly. It's like a home I forgot about."

"Pretty sure I feel asleep as soon as my eyes closed," I admitted.

"How is she doing?" he asked, his smile turning into a frown.

"She's confused and undecided about what she wants to do. I'm hoping that being here this weekend will help her make her decision." What decision she made was definitely going to either be happy or sad for me. Happy if she decided to stay with me beyond the two months. Sad if she confirmed she would return here.

"What if we could get her enrolled into the college?" Porter asked. "I'm sure there are classes she'd be interested in taking there, and I'm sure she could qualify for financial assistance. We both know Coach would put in a good word for her to the admission councilor, too."

Have her attend the college? I hadn't even thought of that.

"Is that what you were talking to her about yesterday?"

He nodded. "I was asking her if she'd ever thought of going to college. She admitted she had wanted to, but earning money to support both her and Marie had been more important."

"I don't want her to sell her house, but I don't think she's going to accept my help financially any more than she already has."

"Or me," Porter added.

I nodded in agreement.

A few of the townspeople walked about their front yards, tending their plants and retrieving their morning newspapers.

"They still read physical papers?" Porter asked.

Laughing, I said, "Yes and there are still teenage boys riding bicycles to deliver them."

"This would be a great place to raise children," he commented. "You and Mollie seemed to turn out okay."

"It's pretty boring when you're a teenager," I admitted. "Not much to do here."

"Are we getting the grand tour today?" he asked, pausing at a turn to look both ways.

"This way," I said and headed left, towards the main street and square. "Yes, we'll give you the grand tour today."

"Let me ask you something," Porter said.

"Uh oh," I muttered.

He laughed. "If you stopped playing hockey tomorrow, how devastated would you be?"

"Because of an injury?" I asked.

Porter shrugged. "For whatever reason."

Thinking about it a moment, I said, "I'd be upset, but I don't know about devastated. I already accepted that I'm not likely to get picked up by the NHL. I want to play as long as I can, though."

He nodded. "I thought that would be your response."

"What about you?" I asked.

"Devastated," he said with a quick nod. He paused at the edge of the town square and whistled at all the booths and decorations. "They go all out, don't they?"

"Wait until tonight," I told him. "It'll be even more extravagant."

We headed back towards Mollie's and he said, "I spoke to Alicia."

My eyes widened. "About?"

"She's offered to help with Mollie's return to figure

skating when she's finished her rehab. She wants to help her out of both a sense of responsibility and because she has faith in Mollie. So, if we can get her to register for college, she can also take lessons with Alicia. Obviously, we need to ask Mollie what she wants to do, but if she does want to go to college, take up figure skating again, and still wants to be a librarian, I think we can make it all happen."

"You know a library she can work at?" I asked with a smirk. "Have you ever been to a library?"

He glared at me. "I get great grades. Anyways, I happen to know the college library hires students part time and I am on good terms with the HR person, since I did some volunteer work for them last year. So, she could get all three of her goals going at the same time."

It was honestly ... perfect. I only wished I had thought of the plan.

"You're scowling. Why are you scowling?"

"Because I think it's perfect for her and now, I'm irritated you thought of it instead of me," I admitted.

He laughed and patted me on the shoulder. "Don't be irritated, just be glad that we're teammates and understand this is what we do. We look out for each other."

CHAPTER 36
Mollie

BRIT SPENT A FULL HOUR ON MY HAIR AND MAKEUP, getting me ready for the Autumn Festival. I'd tried to talk her out of it, but she insisted.

When I'd woken up this morning, Sam and Porter had just returned from a run, both smiling wide and looking delicious as they removed their sweat soaked shirts to reveal sweat soaked six packs.

Brit had made breakfast for everyone and after finishing, Sam drove them around, giving them a tour of the town and some of its landmarks, including ones from our childhood.

We'd eaten lunch at Lucy's, where she had fan girled pretty hard over Porter, who took it well. Brit surprised me by not even being remotely jealous, and smiling and laughing the entire time.

Sam and Porter had been whispering conspiratorially and looking things up on their phones at any opening. I assumed it was related to hockey, but Brit kept asking me questions about the town so I never had a chance to ask.

"I wish I didn't have to use this wheelchair," I complained as I sat in it and watched her getting ready.

"It's either that or Sam carries you, which I think you'd hate more." She snickered at my immediate frown.

"You two almost ready?" Porter asked outside the door.

"Almost!" Brit called back.

"She's lying, it's going to be at least ten more minutes," Porter mumbled.

"Rude!" Brit yelled back. Turning to me she whispered, "But he's right."

Once she was ready, she peeked her head out and said, "Go wait by the car. Porter do what I asked, please."

"What are you talking about?" I asked her.

She just smiled mischievously and waited until she heard the front door shut before pushing me in the wheelchair out of the room and out the front door.

Sam and Porter were both dressed in jeans and button-up shirts, their sleeves rolled back to their elbows. Both had also styled their hair. They looked incredibly handsome.

Sam's eyes widened when he saw me and I self-consciously, tugged at the hem of my dress that rested just above my knees.

Porter whistled. "You look amazing, ladies. Absolutely breathtaking. These country boys won't know what hit 'em." I realized he had his phone out and was videoing Sam. Why?

Sam picked me up out of the wheelchair and kissed me hard on the mouth. "You look gorgeous."

"You look sexy," I admitted and hid my face against his neck.

After setting me down, he buckled my belt and kissed me again, making my toes curl.

"Hurry or we'll be late," Brit complained.

Sam pulled back and kissed my cheek before shutting my door to walk around and get in the front passenger seat.

"Whose fault is that?" Porter teased her.

"Onward!" she said, completely ignoring him.

We drove closer to the town square so we wouldn't have to push my wheelchair as far before exiting.

As soon as we were out and headed down the sidewalk, people began to stop us to talk to Sam and some even to me. Many of the older ladies expressed their sympathies for my injury and their anger at Director Smith. I was both elated and terrified.

Would she keep her decision simply because her name was now tarnished in this town?

I had no doubt she was going to be angry with me.

Brit made the four of us take pictures constantly, but I was okay with it since I didn't have too many pictures with Sam yet. I just wished I wasn't in the cast so I could take one standing with them instead of them squatting down next to me.

While Brit, Porter, and Sam picked out some treats from one of the vendors, I took some time to look around at everyone enjoying the festival.

This was one of my favorite times of year here and one of my favorite events ever.

"How dare you!" Director Smith yelled as she stomped over to me. "You think just because you managed to date Samuel that now you're somehow important? You're nothing more than a drunken whore's pathetic daughter. I gave you that job out of pity, spending months of time training you because you couldn't pick things up, and this is how you repay me?"

Several people nearby turned at her raised voice.

My eyes burned as I kept my tears at bay. I didn't care about her insulting my parents, they were awful people, but she had no right to say anything about me. "I did nothing wrong. You are the one who wrongfully terminated me from a job I was great at. I came up with all of the marketing ideas. I'm the reason the kids started coming back to enjoy the reading times and events. All you did was take credit for it."

"You're banned from the library," she told me. "And don't even think about putting me down for reference checks. I'll tell them what an ungrateful little –"

"That is enough!" Mrs. Abernathy shouted as she walked over, her cane clacking against the concrete. Several other founding ladies followed behind her as well as Sam's mom.

"Mrs. Abernathy!" Director Smith gasped. "I was just—"

"Leaving, I'm sure," Sam's mom said.

"There will be a Board Meeting tomorrow afternoon to decide your fate, Miss Smith. The lack of professionalism you've just displayed is absolutely abhorrent and not what we expect from the director of a library where our grandchildren and great grandchildren go to learn and enjoy themselves."

"You don't understand. She—"

"She was a stellar employee, loved by all of the children and parents, and did absolutely nothing wrong," Mrs. Timberland snapped.

"Did you really come up with all the marketing?" Mrs. Abernathy asked.

I nodded. "And the paint nights and fundraising events."

Sam rushed over and stood behind me, setting his hands on my shoulders. "You okay?"

"Sam, you know me. You know I would never—" Director Smith started, but he cut her off.

He shook his head. "I know that you illegally terminated Mollie and that every student I've talked to adores her. I know that you are a jealous woman who clearly has no respect for others. Look at the scene you've made."

I looked at the expression she had while looking at Sam and the pieces clicked together. "You're jealous," I realized. "You liked Sam and you're jealous that he is dating me, that I was staying with him while recuperating. That's why you fired me."

Her eyes widened and she quickly scoffed and fanned her now red face. "That's absurd!"

Sam sighed and squatted down to hug me from behind. "Once again, I've caused you trouble. I'm sorry, Mol."

I set my hand on his forearm where it lay around my upper chest. "This is not your fault, Sam."

He shook his head and refused to smile the rest of the night.

CHAPTER 37

Mollie

Marie cried as we said our goodbyes, but promised she would fly out for the first game to join me in the box that was reserved for us. Sam's mom had given us each a tin of treats that were filled to the brim.

The flight was just as hard on my leg, but once we were back in Sam's apartment, I lay on the couch and spent the entire afternoon and evening there to recuperate.

"Tomorrow is your checkup appointment," Sam reminded me as he brought out his laptop. "I don't have practice until the afternoon, so I'll take you to it."

"Okay," I agreed.

He spun his laptop towards me and I blinked twice at the PowerPoint presentation on the screen titled, "Mollie's Plan."

"What's this?" I asked.

"Porter and I were talking and we both came to the same conclusion. You have an opportunity before you that you don't know about and so I created this presentation to lay it all out before you."

"You ... created a presentation ... for me?"

He nodded, smiling wide. "It even has animations."

To prove his point, he hit a button and the screen faded out until a new one came tumbling in with the title "Introduction."

I laughed happily as I watched it. No one had ever done something like this for me before.

"May I proceed?"

"Please do!" I nearly shouted.

To my complete shock, he laid out a plan for me to keep my house, do my rehab, stay living with him, go to college, and work in a library all at the same time. The plan was incredibly well thought out, had charts and graphs, and even a proposed class schedule as well as appointment, training, and games included. He also laid out several majors and optional courses he thought I would want to take.

"So, what do you think?" he asked.

Words seemed impossible. What could I say? He'd clearly spent a lot of time working on this and it did sound amazing. But could I really do it? Was it really possible?

"You're concerned about the money, right?"

I nodded.

He hit the next button and I realized the presentation wasn't over. This slide showed an email from the Founding Family Scholarship Foundation stating that if I was accepted to the college, they would give me enough money to cover my tuition, books, and living expenses. Since I was living with Sam, I would be able to use the living expenses portion to pay for my mortgage, and if I got the job at the library, that would provide me pocket cash.

"This ... is real?" I asked.

He nodded. "Mom spoke with them and explained what we wanted and since you had been treated so poorly by Director Smith, they immediately agreed."

"I don't know," I whispered. "That's ..."

"A lot of handouts?" he guessed and I nodded. "I know you don't like getting money from others, but the Founding Family Scholarship Foundation was created specifically for this reason. To help people from the town go to college and accomplish their dreams. They said you can either return to the town and resume your work at the library or you can accept this offer. The choice is up to you."

"My-My job? They'll give me my job back?"

He nodded, though he didn't look happy about it. "If that's what you want, yes." Leaning forward, he took my hands and said, "I want you to do what will make you happy. Yes, I have my opinion about what I'd like you to do, but you can ignore that. You have to decide what you want to do and what will make you happy."

It was a hard choice. On one hand, I would love to return to the library and our town. On the other hand, I had always wanted to take college courses and they even had a minor for creative writing, which was something I hadn't told anyone I was interested in.

"You don't have to answer right now," he said when I continued to stay quiet. "Take your time to decide what you really want to do." He closed the presentation and opened the college's website. "They also have a library sciences major. If you want to continue with your library career. It could help you become a director, if that's something you want."

"Yes," I said immediately. "I want to become director someday."

He smiled and set the laptop on my lap. "Then I suggest you apply."

CHAPTER 38

Sam

My body thrummed with energy as I headed into the locker room for our first game.

Marie had arrived last night. We had gone and picked her up the airport and I'd thoroughly enjoyed watching her and Mollie talk about the latest town drama.

Mollie was so animated when she was with Marie, in a way that she was slowly becoming with Brit, but it was obvious she allowed herself to be completely her when with Marie.

It also stung a little because it made me realize that she wasn't completely herself with me yet. I needed to find a way to make her more comfortable around me and to let her know she didn't need to hide or act different for me. I loved her quirks and silliness.

Mollie, Brit, and Marie were getting ready at my apartment and would arrive together, all three sitting in the box seats that Porter had reserved for them. Mollie had seemed nervous before I left, hugging me extra long and tight.

I assured her that I would be fine. I had pads and a helmet for a reason, but that had only worried her more.

Thankfully, Brit and Marie had spouted off several stats about how rare serious injuries were.

Plus, I wasn't one of the hot heads who got into fights on the ice. Thomspon was the one always fighting on our team due to his cocky mouth. I avoided getting punched as much as possible.

"Tuck!" Porter shouted when he saw me. "You ready to set a new scoring record?"

I bumped my forearm against his and smiled wide. "You know it!" I'd told him about my bet with Mollie, something I was determined to win.

"He's got to show off for his lady," Thompson said and snickered. "I never thought I'd see the day that Tucker turned into a purse carrying simp for a girl."

"You're just jealous because my girl is amazing and the only girls you attract are ones that require you to get tested every month," I replied.

The locker room filled with "Ohh"s.

"Heads in the game!" Coach snapped as he entered. He turned a glare on me and said, "Get suited up, Tucker."

I realized I was the last one not dressed. "Yes, sir," I said, and hurried to get changed.

The next thirty minutes were a blur as I got ready and we listened to Coach's reminders. My mind also returned again and again to the bet. Mollie had seemed excited about the bet we'd made, something unusual for her. It made me hopeful that she truly was going to stay with me and go to college here as well. Mrs. Abernathy had really set things in motion with the scholarship offer. I knew I had Mom to thank for that and would buy her a big gift soon.

We skated out onto the ice and some of my nerves disappeared. The familiar location and movements allowed me to settle as I skated once around the rink and to my position. Every game was nerve wracking, and I was full of anxiety until we started playing. Once we started though, all of that went out the window as I focused.

My eyes went to the box and I smiled when I found Mollie standing up at the window, wearing my jersey, and with my number painted on her face.

"What you lookin' at, Tuck Butt?" Anderson, the biggest douche on our rivals, the Northwest Wolverines, asked. "You finally stop sucking off Porter and find a puck bunny?"

He was trying to get a rise out of me, like he always did, but I ignored him. Ignoring him would piss him off more than any reply.

Taking a breath, I calmed my thoughts.

The puck dropped and all of my focus went to it. My extra training sessions had definitely paid off. Within minutes, I slapped the puck into the net.

The crowd erupted in screams and cheers.

I raised my stick, pointed it at Mollie, and thumped my hand against my chest.

She made a heart with her hands in response, making me smile even wider.

CHAPTER 39

Mollie

Watching Sam play was simultaneously thrilling and terrifying.

Brit and Marie assured me he was going to be fine, but I still worried.

I had leapt to my feet when he made the goal, glad I no longer had my cast on and could. Though, I wobbled a bit since I had a brace on.

When he pointed at me and thumped his chest, my heart fluttered.

I felt like the luckiest woman in the world.

I made a heart with my hands in response, since he couldn't hear me.

"Oh my god, I think I must swooned," Marie gasped.

I sat back down and took a big drink of my water, fanning my face.

Looking down into the stands, I found many glares pointed in my direction.

"Ignore the haters. They're all just jealous because you're the first girl he's scored for," Brit said.

A loud siren went off as Sam scored a second goal, once again pointing at me and thumping his chest over his heart and then holding up two fingers.

"Girl, what bet did you make before the game?" Brit asked.

"Bet?" Marie asked.

"All players make a bet with their girls, or the girl they plan to see after, about the game," she explained.

My face warmed as I answered, "If he scores six goals, I'll enroll in college here and accept the scholarship I was offered."

"What?" both shrieked.

What none of them knew was that I'd already accepted and the college allowed me to sign up for a late start class that began in two weeks.

The siren sounded again, but this time Porter was the scorer.

He pointed his stick at our box and Brit's hands flew to her mouth. "He really did it."

"What?" I asked.

"He said he was tired of us being just bed buddies. That he wanted to be official. I bet that he had to make a goal for me and I would agree. He never ..." Her eyes filled with tears. "... he has never been serious about any girl. Never pointed to any of us who shared his bed." She turned to me and threw her arms around me. "Thank you. It's all thanks to the trip to your town and seeing you and Tucker together. I've been waiting two years for this."

I patted her back and said, "It's because of you being an awesome person."

"Back up to you agreeing to go to college here," Marie said once Brit released me.

I explained everything to them, including my goal of becoming the director of the library in our town when I returned.

"I'm so happy for you, but so sad you'll be away from me so long," Marie said with a pout.

"We have this box every home game," I informed her.

"And you can stay with me whenever you want," Brit offered. "I know Sam's apartment is small."

"That would be great. I feel bad making him sleep on the couch," Marie replied and we all laughed. "You'll come home for the holidays, right?" she asked.

I nodded. "One of the nice things about Sam and I being from the same town."

The alarm sounded, pulling our attention back to the game.

"A hat trick!" Brit shouted.

Sam held up three fingers and blew me a kiss with them. A sign for his goals and a sign from one of my favorite movies.

"Oh, my ovaries," Marie groaned.

"Ditto," I whispered and pretended to catch his kiss.

"Oh! You're on the screen!" Marie gasped.

I looked up and my face erupted in flames of embarrassment to find them splitting my face with Sam's on the jumbotron screen.

CHAPTER 40

Sam

As soon as I stepped out of the locker room, an uneasy feeling hit me.

Rushing down the hallway and around the corner, I saw I had been right.

Three reporters had Mollie trapped in a corner.

Reaching between them, I tugged her free and wrapped her in a tight hug. "There you are, beautiful."

She exhaled shakily and her hands fisted the back of my shirt.

"Tucker, congratulations on your best game yet. Do you have any comments for your fans?"

"Tucker, is this your girlfriend?"

"How does it feel to tie the most goals in one game?"

They shouted off their questions so fast I didn't have time to answer if I wanted to.

"You okay?" I whispered in her ear.

She looked up and smiled. "Congrats on winning the game and our bet." Reaching into her bag, she pulled out her phone and showed me her class schedule that started in two weeks. My eyes widened at the date of the email ... one week ago.

"You'd already accepted! You brat." I tickled her side and smiled wider at her adorable laugh.

"Well, the bet worked, didn't it? You scored your most goals ever in a single game. It was quite impressive."

"How impressive?" I asked, my voice dropping lower as I pulled her flush against my body.

Her cheeks reddened and she whispered, "Sam, there are reporters behind us."

Oh, right.

Tucking her against my side, a protective arm around her shoulders, I faced them.

"Sorry, what were your questions?"

The three looked completely unfazed by my dismissiveness.

"Oh, right. I'm proud of the way our team played today and look forward to winning the cup this year."

"And will your girlfriend be at all the games?" one asked.

I smiled down at her as she looked up at me. "As many as I can convince her to attend." I tugged on the arm of the jersey she wore. "There's no better feeling than seeing you in the stands in my jersey. Makes me want to score as many goals as possible to be able to see you as much as I can while playing."

"What's your name, miss?"

"Mollie," she answered.

"Excuse us," I said before they could ask more. "We've got to go meet my captain and we all know he hates waiting."

As we walked out of the building a few girls loitered, waiting to try to talk to players.

One skipped forward. "Sam! You played great. Are you busy later?"

Mollie glared at her. "Yea, he's busy later."

My eyes widened. She never would have said something before. Maybe Brit was rubbing off on her.

"Call me if you change your mind," the girl said.

"I won't," I replied and squeezed Mollie as we continued walking to the car.

"That was hot," I told her as we buckled our seat belts.

She huffed out a laugh. "I can't believe how brazen they are. I'm literally on your arm!"

I leaned over, kissed her cheek, and set my hand on her leg. "Don't worry. I'm not a fan of brazen women. I like mine shy, nerdy, and into naughty books."

"Steamy, not naughty," she corrected and smiled, but her cheeks reddened again. "Come on, we've got to get to Porter's."

"You? Excited for a party?" I fake gasped.

"No, I just don't want to leave Brit and Marie alone too long or they might start trouble."

Laughing, I said, "Those two are trouble with a capital T and we both know you'll just get dragged into their shenanigans."

She shrugged. "Only one way to find out."

CHAPTER 41
Mollie

My life had turned into a whirlwind. I woke up at five a.m., worked out with Sam, went to three classes, worked at the library for four hours, went to physical therapy, ate dinner with Sam, showered, and slept.

I didn't even get a reprieve on the weekends because I spent most of it doing homework or traveling with Brit for the guys' away games.

We pulled into the hotel parking lot for the weekend's game and I breathed a sigh of relief. "I need a bath."

Brit wafted her nose. "Yeah, you do."

We both laughed as we climbed out and retrieved our suitcases from the trunk.

Arms wrapped around my stomach and lifted me off my feet.

I squealed and thrashed, trying to break free.

"Hey! It's me!" Sam shouted and set me back down.

Sighing, I sagged forward before turning to face him. "You scared ten years off my life, Samuel Tucker!"

He smiled, unashamed, and kissed my cheek. "Sorry, darlin'. I was just so excited to see you. I've missed you."

"It's only been one week," Brit said and shook her head.

"Which is long enough to make anyone miss their girl," Porter said as he joined us, sliding his arms around her waist and kissing her on the top of her head.

She melted into him and I couldn't help smiling wider at how adorable they were. Ever since he had publicly made his intentions clear, they'd been inseparable, and he'd turned up the charm, which had her melting all over again for him.

"How's your shoulder?" I asked Sam. He'd gotten hit really hard at the last game and had admitted it bothered him a bit even a week later.

"It's better," he said.

Porter looked over with a frown. "The shoulder from last game is still bothering you? Why didn't you say anything?"

"It's nothing," Sam replied quickly.

"I'm telling Marsden tomorrow." Porter looked at me. "In the future, tell me anytime he whines about an injury. He keeps that to himself too long and ends up needing PT. I'm not letting him lose out this year."

"I'll be sure to rat him out sooner in the future," I promised with a smile at Porter, earning me a scowl from Sam.

"Your mom called me," I said to distract him.

"About?"

"Apparently, someone broke into my house," I admitted.

Everyone went completely still a moment and then bombarded me with questions.

I raised my hands in the air. "Bobby Rae installed security cameras and a new system and Mrs. Thompson who lives next door is going to keep a closer eye on things."

"No leads?" Sam asked.

I shook my head and rubbed my arms. Even though I hadn't been there, it still bothered me. Why would someone break into my house? We weren't like big towns that had people breaking in and there wasn't much to steal since I didn't live there.

"I'll do some research online," Brit said.

"For what?" I asked.

She, Sam, and Porter all exchanged looks.

"Just ... to see if anything pops up," she answered vaguely.

I gave her my best mean glare, both to let her know I knew she was bullshitting and as a promise that I would bring it up later when the guys weren't around.

"Come on, let's get you ladies inside and checked in," Sam said, smiling and slipping his arm around my waist to pull me along. "After you get checked in, we've got Chinese food in our room since we figured you would be hungry."

"Famished!" I shouted and squeezed him. "Thanks for thinking of me."

"Always."

After checking in, eating, chatting, and catching up, we separated to our room to sleep. It had been a very long drive and I desperately needed some rest before the hecticness of their game tomorrow.

As I brushed my teeth, pajamas on, my phone pinged. I gasped as I pulled up the live feed of my front door where a very haggard looking Tiffany was trying to pry open my door.

"Is that Tiffany?" Brit gasped over my shoulder.

"I-I think so. How did she get my address? Why is she there? What is she doing?" I spouted the questions fast, my brain malfunctioning.

"Call the cops, hun," she urged me.

I turned off the feed and called Sherriff Brunson on his personal cell, since I knew it was too late for him to be at the office still.

"Mollie? What is it?" he asked, groaning and obviously having been woken by my call.

"The girl who broke my leg is currently trying to break into my house," I said quickly.

"What?" he snapped. "You mean the Victorian here?"

"Yes, my security camera shows she's trying to open my front door right now."

"Where are you?" he demanded, his voice much clearer now that he was awake and knew it was police related.

"I'm in a different state, attending one of Sam's away games."

He exhaled. "Good. I'll head over right now and let you know what happens. If we apprehend her, you want to press charges?"

"Only if she actually did something. Not sure if she managed to break in since I stopped watching the feed to call you."

"I'll call you tomorrow. Get some rest and let us here take care of it, you hear?"

"Yes, sir," I replied automatically.

I hung up and didn't realize I was shaking until Brit wrapped her arms around me.

"Do you want me to call the guys?" she asked.

Shaking my head, I took several deep breaths to calm

myself. "No, I don't want this to affect their game tomorrow. I'll tell them after. For now, let's try to go to bed."

When we walked out of the bathroom, I stared at the two separate beds.

Sensing my hesitation, Brit asked, "You want to share a bed? I know she's states away, but I also know if it were me, I wouldn't want to feel alone right now."

I nodded. "Please."

She hugged me and said, "We're friends, Mollie Lollie. This is part of what we do. Now, do you want big spoon or little spoon?"

Laughing at her joke, I climbed into the bed with her and felt better already. "Thank you, for being my friend."

She patted my head before turning off the light and said, "Ditto."

CHAPTER 42

Sam

Winning the game had been great, we were on our way to the championship for sure with how well we were playing, but my shoulder was hurting more than I liked to admit since I'd gotten hit once again.

One of those jerks on the other side had slammed me extra hard into the wall, their arm digging into my shoulder on purpose, no doubt.

Cap had ratted me out to the coach and the physical therapist, but I had still lied about how much it actually hurt me right now.

I couldn't afford to be put on the bench. Not yet. Not while we were so close.

I had to get through this season and secure us a cup before I retired.

If I got put on the bench, I wouldn't get to fulfill my dream of winning the cup at least once during my time on this team. Plus, I wouldn't ever get drafted. Not that I was sure that was really what I wanted anyway, but I would like to be asked at least once.

Sneaking back to my room, I had filled the tub with ice and lay in it while I knew Cap would be taking the girls out for a dinner. I'd convinced them that I needed to speak to a few people and do interviews to give myself time alone.

I hated lying to Mollie, but I knew she would rat me out if I didn't.

My phone rang, Mom calling me to congratulate me on the game, but I ignored it.

Once I was done with my ice bath, I would respond.

A loud bang had me jerking upright in the tub.

"Don't worry, Sam's busy with interviews," Cap said as he entered the room.

"I don't want to leave Mollie alone too long. It's not safe," Brit whispered.

Crap! They'd come back to the room not knowing I was here. This was really uncomfortable.

While I could stay here, silently, while they had their fun, at some point they were likely to come in here once they finished.

What should I do?

What was the best option?

As soon as I pulled the plug on the tub, they would hear it draining.

Dammit, I hated this entire situation.

This was one of the worst possible outcomes of the night.

My phone vibrated on the counter and I quickly grabbed it so they wouldn't hear it.

Mollie had messaged me.

Mollie: Do you know how much longer you'll be? I'm bored and lonely without you. 🥺

She'd sent a picture with it, one of her on the bed in lingerie.

She had never sent me a provocative picture before.

Dammit!

My dream was coming true and I was stuck in this hotel bathroom!

No!

"Did you hear that?" Brit asked from the room.

Crap!

Quickly, I messaged Mollie back and climbed out of the tub.

Me: I'll be there in 2 🏃,

No other recourse available, I pulled the plug and dried myself off. I wrapped the towel around my waist and stepped out of the room, eyes wide at Brit and Cap on the bed. "Oh. Sorry. I wanted to clean myself off after the game. I didn't realize you'd come back. Don't worry, I'm leaving."

Porter's eyes narrowed on me, but Brit saved me.

"Well, you better hurry. Pretty sure your girl is next door all alone and vulnerable. You should go protect her."

I saluted her, grabbed some clothes to put on, and said, "Thanks for the tip, Brit. Have fun you two."

I took the clothes back to the bathroom and changed faster than I ever had before.

CHAPTER 43

Mollie

SAM LAY ASLEEP ON THE BED BESIDE ME, HIS GAME AND our lovemaking had worn him out, and he now snored softly, mouth hanging open.

Even though I should have been tired, too, I couldn't shake the uneasy feeling in my gut. Even though she was states away and locked up in the city jail, I couldn't stop thinking about Tiffany.

"Babe?" Sam asked, his voice groggy with sleep. He sat up and rubbed his eyes before embracing me in a tight hug with one arm around my waist and the other around my chest, wrapping me in a cocoon of warmth. "What's wrong?" He rubbed the tip of his nose behind my ear and placed a soft kiss against the sensitive skin, making me shiver.

"Nothing, go back to sleep," I said quickly and tried to disentangle myself and slide out of bed, but he tightened his grip.

"Mollie, what's wrong?" he blinked, turned me around so he could look into my eyes. Once he looked at me more clearly, he fully woke up as he realized I was uneasy about something.

Sighing, I rested my head against his shoulder and admitted, "So, a thing happened I didn't tell you about because I didn't want it to affect your game. I even made your mama promise not to say anything."

He released me and sat up fully. His hair was sticking out all over the place and seeing him so disheveled while looking at me so seriously eased a bit of the tension in my gut.

"Tell me."

Taking a breath, I told him about Tiffany breaking into my house and getting arrested. She hadn't done more than break in because I'd notified Sherriff Brunson so quickly and because Mrs. Thompson had heard the noise and came to investigate. However, Tiffany wouldn't admit how she'd gotten my address or why she'd been trying to break in to begin with. She had had a lighter on her, but swore it was because she smoked.

Sam paced in front of the bed in the small hotel room, scowling and tugging at the strings of his pajama pants. "I don't know how or why she'd have done it, either. It makes no sense."

"I think that's what bothers me the most," I admitted. "The not knowing."

He sat beside me and hugged me again. "I'm glad you're with me and weren't home."

"Me, too," I admitted and wrapped my arms around him, hugging him tightly. "What if she comes to your apartment next? Or your next game? She knows where to find you."

"I'll make sure to add her to the banned list with security for our home games and let the guards at the apartment complex know about her as well," he replied immediately. "We'll institute a buddy system so neither of us is alone, okay?"

I nodded. "Okay."

My stomach growled and he reached down to pat it. "Sounds like it's dinner time. You shouldn't have let me sleep when you haven't eaten yet."

We separated to get dressed and I shrugged. "You looked like you needed the sleep and I'm not going to die from not eating for a couple of hours."

Instead of ordering room service, we went to the hotel's restaurant. Just as we sat, Brit and Porter joined us.

"Seems like our stomachs are on the same schedule," Brit joked.

I nodded. "Seems that way!"

Sam was focused on his phone and Porter leaned over to see what he was doing. Porter's eyes widened and he looked up at me. "Tiffany broke into your house?"

Setting the menu down, I nodded. "Yes, she was arrested for breaking and entering. We still don't know why she did it. She won't admit any reason."

"I knew she was crazy, but this is some next level craziness," he said and shook his head.

"Hello, what can I get started for you?" our waiter, a beautiful Latina woman in her late thirties or early forties asked. Her curly hair was pulled back into a ponytail with the curls framing her perfectly.

"I love your hair," I admitted and then covered my mouth. "Sorry, that just came out."

She laughed and said, "I get that all the time, girl! Thank you."

"I'll have a club sandwich with fries and a coke," I ordered and felt my cheeks burning.

Brit smirked, entertained by my embarrassing interaction. "House salad with ranch and a beer," she ordered.

"Actually, can I have a beer, too?" I asked, changing my drink order.

"Sure thing, hun," the waitress agreed. She turned to Sam and asked, "What about you, handsome?"

"Fish tacos and beer, too, since it seems to be popular," he said without looking up from his phone.

"I'll have same as him," Porter ordered. "But double the tacos, please. Got to feed all these muscles."

The waitress laughed and took our menus. "You hockey players and your massive appetites. I can never get enough of it. I'll be right back with your beers."

Sam finally put his phone down and looked at me. "Promise you won't hide things from me in the future?"

"I wasn't hiding it," I countered. "I just didn't want you distracted during your game."

"We appreciate that, but when it comes to you two ladies' safety, that takes precedence," Porter said. "If you see her, you let us know immediately."

"Even if you're in a game?" I teased.

"Especially if we're in a game," Porter replied immediately.

"And how would we do that?" I asked, rolling my eyes. "Run up to the glass and scream at you?"

"That'd work," Sam agreed.

Brit rolled her eyes. "You're being a bit over the top now, you two."

"No, over the top would be me hiring bodyguards, which

isn't out of the question yet," Porter said. "If she shows up near either of you, I'll do just that."

My eyes nearly bugged out of my face. "You're crazy," I whispered.

"No, the crazy thing is you thinking that we won't do whatever we need to in order to keep you safe," Sam said. "Had she shown up here or at the college, I would have sent you back to stay with Mama, but now I'm going to keep you closer just to be safe."

"I don't know, Mollie. A couple of sexy bodyguards protecting us with their lives might not be such a bad deal," Brit teased.

Porter scowled at her. "Joke all you want, babe, but now that you're mine, I'm going to do whatever I need to to keep you happy, healthy, and safe."

Her eyes widened and her cheeks reddened. "Mollie's right, you guys are being over the top."

"She didn't even do anything," I said quickly. "Hopefully, she'll just leave me alone and we'll never see or hear from her again."

"Let's hope so," Sam said, "but promise you'll let us know if you hear from her or see her?"

Brit and I crossed our hearts and simultaneously said, "Promise."

"I don't know what you're promising, but seems like I should get you a second round right away," the waitress said as she set our beer glasses down. "I'll go put that order in now."

"Change it to a pitcher and add an order of onion rings!" Brit called out.

The waitress gave her a thumbs up. "Yes, girl! You got it!"

CHAPTER 44

Sam

MOLLIE WAS TRYING TO PRETEND THE TIFFANY THING hadn't happened and acting like everything was fine. While I was okay with her doing it to ease her mind and not be stressed, I was not letting it go.

Mom had assured me that the town members were all well aware of Tiffany and that she was crazy. She'd also assured me that she had spread word to everyone to not give out any information about me or Mollie. There were plenty of other crazy fans out there and we didn't need more people learning about Mollie's address or trying to do anything else insane.

News articles about the breaking and entering had been vague, but most people figured out it was related to me and Mollie. A few fans had made comments suggesting that they'd considered doing similar things before and that chill down my spine hadn't left since reading those comments.

Mollie opted not to press charges despite Porter and my adamant objections and so Tiffany was free and out in the world. She thought it would make Tiffany give up, see that she wasn't her enemy, but it worried me more.

Months went by with nothing happening and thankfully we kept winning our games. My shoulder was getting worse, though, but I hid it the best I could as we approached the championship game.

We had to win this final game and then we'd be in the championship. No matter what happened, I had to focus up and help the team win.

This entire situation had really forced me to assess my priorities and I knew my decision, even if I hadn't told anyone else about it yet. Some things were just too important in our short lives to put to chance. I was working silently to set it all into motion without Porter or Mollie knowing yet.

"You okay?" Mollie asked as I tied my shoes, my bag on the floor next to me as I prepared to head out for our final game.

"Yeah, just a bit anxious since this game decides if we make it to the championship or not," I said and smiled up at her.

She stood before me in my jersey and a skirt that was short enough it almost disappeared beneath the hem of the jersey. Her makeup was done beautifully and her hair was swept up into a messy bun that reminded me she was my sexy little librarian.

I pulled her down onto my lap and kissed her hard, our tongues tangling together and her arms wrapping tightly around my neck until we broke apart, panting. "You're staying here until Brit and Marie pick you up, right?"

She nodded. "Door locked and me safely inside until both of them arrive."

I squeezed her and kissed her hard on the lips again. "I'm going to score as many goals for you as I can."

"Do your best, that's all anyone can expect from you. Now ..." she stood, pulled me to my feet, and swatted my but, "... go win the game!"

Chuckling, I grabbed my bag and slung it over my shoulder. "Yes, ma'am."

After one more kiss, I headed outside, where Porter was waiting for me in his truck. "Ready to win this?" he asked and bumped fists with me.

"You know it!"

He shouted and started the vehicle. "Let's win this thing and the championship! We'll show everyone that we're the best players!"

"The best team!"

He nodded and his energy spread to me. By the time we reached the locker room, we were both vibrating with excitement.

No matter what happened in the future, today, I was going to win this game and show Mollie exactly what she meant to me. I couldn't wait to see her face.

CHAPTER 45
Mollie

Brit used our secret knock right at six o'clock. The knock was one that Porter had required us to develop, a precaution so I didn't open the door to trouble.

I double checked the peephole to be sure it was her as well. While I wasn't paranoid like Porter, a little extra safety never hurt anyone.

Opening the door, I gasped as Marie stepped out from behind Brit and threw her arms around me.

Both of us squealed in excitement, dancing around while holding onto each other.

"What are you doing here?" I asked and stepped back to see her. She was dressed in Porter's jersey and a cute, swishy, black skirt.

Brit also wore Porter's jersey, but it didn't look like she had anything beneath.

"You think I'm going to miss the last semifinal game?" She scoffed. "Not a chance!"

"You look adorable," Brit praised. "Your makeup and hair game have definitely improved over the last year."

"Thanks," I replied. "I felt it was sort of necessary since I keep ending up on social media or the jumbotron and don't want to embarrass Sam."

Marie rolled her eyes. "You could show up in a potato sack and he wouldn't care. It's obvious that boy is head over heels in love with you."

Brit nodded her agreement and a huge smile split my face.

They were right. I knew not just from the way he said it, but from all of the little things he did.

I was deeply in love with him, too. So deep that all my future plans were no longer certain or decided. While I had spent the majority of my life pre-planning everything, I now found myself planning simply to wait and see what Sam decided and pivot to what his goals were.

Grabbing my cards and keys, I quickly pushed the girls out into the hallway. "Come on, I don't want to be stuck in parking traffic any longer than I have to be."

"You just want to get there early enough to watch their on ice stretches," Marie teased.

I laughed and said, "Don't lie, you love watching them, too."

"Who wouldn't? They're practically advertising how good they must be in bed," Marie said.

"Can attest!" Brit said, earning a tickling from Marie for bragging.

Parking took much longer than normal, which made sense, since this was such an important game.

Finally, we made it to our reserved box, but sadly we'd missed warmups.

We got our snacks and drinks, posted obligatory selfies on social media, and sat to watch the game.

"I feel nervous. Why do I feel nervous?" Brit asked and chugged her drink. "I've never felt this nervous for a game before."

"Because you are officially with Porter now," I answered. "Because I feel the same."

"They've got this," Marie said confidently. "They've never played better than this year. It's their year."

As the players skated out onto the ice, Sam and Porter side by side, raised their sticks and pointed at our box.

I made a heart with my hands and Brit blew Porter three kisses back to back.

It wasn't surprising to see our images upon the jumbotron in the next second. The crowd cheered, but I knew it was for Sam and Porter, their star players.

The game started and I sat, transfixed, as the teams battled. Intense didn't even begin to describe it. After the first period, the score was still zero-zero.

We refilled our drinks, got more snacks, and used the restroom during the intermission between periods. None of us wanted to miss a second of the game.

Someone knocked on the door to our box and after the three of us exchanged worried glances, Brit went and opened it.

She immediately stepped back to let two male security officers wearing stadium uniforms and name badges in. they were both over thirty, but one looked over fifty.

"Evening," The older of the two greeted us.

"Is there a security concern?" Brit asked. "Has Tiffany been spotted here?"

"No, nothing like that. You've no need for worry. The coach asked us to be here and to escort you three to special seats before the end of the game to make it easier to see the team. Since this is a tense game and you two especially are well known, we want to ease Porter's and Tucker's minds as well as ensure your safety. It's all just precautionary."

Marie, Brit, and I all exhaled in relief.

The younger of the two frowned and asked, "Is there a specific person we should be on the lookout for?"

Brit showed them a picture of Tiffany and explained all about my broken leg and the breaking and entering.

"We'll be right outside the door, so don't worry. We won't let any unauthorized people enter. You three enjoy the game."

Once they were out and we returned to our seats, I turned to Brit and asked, "Do you think they're hiding something?"

She shrugged. "I don't know, but I am going to believe them and focus back on the game. Honestly, it makes me feel safer with them out there. I was worried about getting out to the guys after the game ends. Plus, we both know how over protective and stressed Porter's been about our safety lately."

"I can see Sam asking them to assign security officers to you," Marie added.

Since both seemed unconcerned, I let it go. They were probably right.

The game started again, further distracting me. A few minutes later, Sam scored a goal, the first of the game.

I leapt to my feet, screaming along with the other Westwood Raven fans in the stadium, our excitement shared.

Sam turned and pounded his chest twice before pointing at me.

The battle continued for two more periods and we approached the final period, too close to call.

"Ladies, if you'll follow me, we will get you down to the team safely," the younger security officer said.

"It's not over yet," I said in confusion.

"Moving now makes it easier before the crowds push against us," he explained.

I finished my glass of champagne and followed between Brit and Marie, the older security officer leading and the younger bringing up the rear.

Brit and Marie were smiling ear to ear, so I brushed aside my nervousness and followed.

They lead us down to three empty seats right behind the team's box.

Paolo, one of the players, turned and winked at us, earning an eye roll from Brit.

"He's such a flirt," she said and shook her head.

The fierce competition continued, but in the end, we won with a two to one score, thanks to a goal by Porter in the final period!

The stadium filled with roaring fans as the Westwood Ravens won and secured their spot in the final game. One step closer to the championship.

The other team left the ice, but Sam and his teammates stayed.

Shocking me, the announcer said, "Fans, friends, and families of the Westwood Ravens. We have an exciting finale, so please stay in your seats a moment longer, please."

"What's going on?" I asked Brit.

She was practically bouncing in her seat as she said, "You'll see in a second. But put these on." She handed me my ice skates and my eyes nearly flew out of my skull.

Still, I obeyed and put them on.

"Miss Mollie West, please report to the security officer nearest you. Again, Miss Mollie West, please report to the security officer nearest you."

My eyes widened as I automatically stood and both Brit and Marie shoved me towards the younger security officer who had escorted us.

They opened the door so I could step out onto the ice and I obeyed numbly, so uncertain and shocked that I simply followed orders.

Porter skated over, grabbed my shoulders, and pushed me towards the center of the ice where Sam and the announcer stood.

"What is going on?" I demanded, my heart pounding.

Sam smiled wide at me as I neared and took my hand when I was close enough.

The announcer held the microphone to Sam's mouth as he began to speak.

"Mollie, I have been in love with you since junior high when we had a science project together. You are the sweetest, smartest, and most beautiful soul on this planet. I love you more than anything in this world, even my mama's cookies."

The crowd chuckled.

"Will you do me the honor of becoming my wife?"

The crowd, myself included, gasped.

Holding the microphone up to me, the announcer, Sam, and everyone else waited for my answer.

It had formed as soon as he started speaking, so I swallowed hard before nodding and answering, "Yes"

Sam surged to his feet, kissing me hard before putting the gorgeous ring on my finger.

The crowd erupted in screams and cheers, none louder than my two girls.

Sam linked hands with me and we skated in a circle around the rink, waving to the fans.

"Now the Westwood Ravens will have two things to celebrate this year!" the announcer yelled. "Thank you for joining us on this beautiful journey."

CHAPTER 46

Sam

"Explain it to me like I'm five years old," Porter ordered me as he folded his arms and narrowed his eyes.

I sat across from him at the dining table in his house. The rest of our teammates sat at the table or surrounded us, all wanting to hear what was going on and why I needed a super secret meeting with Porter without any of the media or coach nearby to hear us.

"That's how I explain everything to you," I replied with a smile.

He didn't react. Not even a glare or narrowing of eyes.

Exhaling, I grabbed my beer can, took a swing, and said, "After the championship, I am retiring from hockey, finishing my degree, and moving back to my small town to marry and live with Mollie. I will be Director of Marketing and Outreach for my uncle's company, so I'll be fully utilizing my college degree and earning a good salary."

"Have you talked to Mollie about this?" Porter asked. "Does she even want to go back to your small town when she hasn't finished her degree yet? Or gotten the experience from the library on campus to push her to becoming Director?"

Dropping my eyes, I shook my head, but I quickly raised it. "No, I haven't talked to her yet, but I do know she wants to move back once she finishes her degree." At least, I was pretty sure she did.

"But you're going to retire from hockey this year? Even though you'll still be going here next year?" Tony asked.

I nodded.

"Your shoulder is worse than you're letting on, isn't it?" Porter asked, his eyes focused on the offending body part.

My hand immediately reached up to touch my shoulder. "I've got one more game in me. Don't worry about the championship."

"I'm not worried about that. I'm worried about you and Mollie."

Porter and I hadn't been close at the beginning of the year, but now I considered him my closest friend on the team and in life. It was crazy how much could change in a year.

"Well, it's obvious that the first thing you need to do is talk to Mollie and find out what she wants to do," Porter said. "And the second thing you need to do, after our game, is go to the doctor for your shoulder."

"Are you going to invite us to your wedding?" Marco asked.

"Yeah!" Tony shouted. "I want to see your home town and meet your mom to thank her for all the cookies she sends us."

"I just proposed yesterday," I reminded them. "Wedding plans haven't been discussed yet."

"Oh, they're being discussed, just not with you," Porter

said and laughed. "Brit bought her a wedding planning binder, Marie bought a dozen wedding magazines, and the three women are deep into it already. That's what they've been doing all day."

"So, it's Mollie I need to text to ensure I get an invite. Tucker, give me Mollie's phone number," Tony said and held out his hand like I was going to put her number in it.

"There is a zero percent chance I would ever give you my girl's number," I said and stood. "Now, I've got to get home so I can talk to Mollie before Cap and Brit plan my wedding and my future for me without allowing my input."

"Too late," Porter called after me. "You gave me that power when you asked me to be your best man."

"Clearly a mistake on my part," I said as I opened the front door.

"No takesies backsies," he said in a sing-song tone as I walked out.

CHAPTER 47
Mollie

THE DIAMOND ON MY FINGER REFLECTED SUNLIGHT INTO my eyes, distracting me for the thirtieth time that day.

Part of me was still in disbelief that the ring on my finger, that the events yesterday, had truly happened.

I, Mollie West, was engaged. Engaged to Sam Tucker, my school crush, and star player of the Westwood Ravens.

Brit and Marie sat across from me, ripping pages out of bridal magazines, making notes in the wedding binder, and putting together a plan I knew I would love. All while I tried to accept this was real life.

"Do I need me to pinch you again?" Marie asked.

I rubbed the spot on my arm I was certain would be bruised tomorrow. "No."

Brit snickered. "The shock will wear off soon."

"Knowing her, it'll wear off just after their tenth anniversary," Marie muttered.

I threw a pillow at her, but she deflected it with ease.

The front door unlocked and Sam walked in.

Nerves crackled within me for some reason and I felt like I had on our second date.

He smiled at me and walked over to kiss the top of my head. "Hello, beautiful." He looked over Marie's shoulder and pointed at one of the pictures in the magazine she was currently flipping through. "I like that."

"Oh, good choice, Tuck," Brit praised and tore the page out to add it to the growing pile at her side.

"Mollie, can I steal you for a bit?" he asked.

My throat tightened. Was he already having second thoughts? Had he changed his mind about us?

"S-Sure," I said, put on my shoes, grabbed my bag with my cards, and followed him.

Instead of getting into the car, we walked down the street to one of my favorite cafes.

He ordered food while I snagged a table in the back corner, trying to find a spot for a bit of privacy if he was going to dump me.

My leg bounced erratically as I wanted for him to sit so we could talk.

When he sat, he immediately reached across and gripped one of my hands. "Stop your bad thoughts. Our talk isn't me taking back the ring. I one hundred percent plan on marrying you and giving you my last name."

Breath whooshed out of my lungs and I dropped my head to rest on one of my arms.

"I wanted to talk about the future, *our* future. About what happens after we graduate," he explained.

Sitting back up, I met his calm gaze with a wild one. "Did you get recruited by the NHL?" it would make sense with how well he'd been playing and that he was playing in the final game.

He shook his head. "No. Actually, I ... well, first what is it that you want to do after you get your degree?"

I shrugged. "I was mostly waiting to see what happens with you and your hockey career."

His eyes widened, he released my hand, and he sat back to stare at me. "You really are too good for me, Mollie West."

I rolled my eyes at him, but my reply was cut off by Patty, the café owner, bringing us our food and drinks. "Congratulations on your engagement," she said with a huge smile. "I knew you two were meant to be."

"Thanks, Patty," I replied and Sam thanked her as well.

"I'm retiring," Sam said suddenly, distracting me from putting ketchup on my burger.

"What?" My eyes darted to his shoulder, the one that had been giving him trouble, and narrowed. "How bad is it? Do I need to call—"

"I'm playing the last game and retiring," he explained. "It's not good, but not awful. The main reason is that I don't really ever plan to go pro, and because I want to move back, with you. But I realized that I have never asked you what you *want* to do. So, what do you want?"

My brows furrowed as I thought about it. "Part of me wants to stay here, nearby, but honestly ..." Taking a breath, I admitted. "I want to go home. I want to go back to my Victorian and try to become Director of the library there."

He smiled and said, "Then let's do it. Let's go home, Mollie."

CHAPTER 48

Sam

MOLLIE LAY SNUGGLED AGAINST ME, HER HEAD ON MY chest, and her fingers trailing up and down my arm, pausing every so often on my shoulder. "You're going to be careful, right?"

I smiled against her hair and nodded as I squeezed her around the waist. "Yes, I'm going to be careful. The last thing I want is to get injured seriously before our wedding."

A wedding that was happening in just a couple of weeks. When we video called Mom and told her about the engagement, she'd gone ballistic, cheering, crying, and laughing. It wasn't long until she was on daily video calls with Brit and Marie, helping to plan our wedding. And, true to their reputation, the town's women all got involved as well.

Mollie was relieved about the stress being taken from her, though I knew she was stressing the most about her wedding dress.

"How goes your dress search?" I asked.

She huffed out a breath. "As well as it was two days ago. I've got a ton of ideas, styles I like, designs I like, and places to

go, but there's just ... too many. I did schedule an appointment for Saturday to try on some dresses. Marie thinks me
actually trying them on will help me decide."

"I think she's right," I agreed. "When you see yourself in
the dress, you'll find one you love, one that makes you feel
like the queen you are."

She shifted and I knew if I could see her face that she'd
be blushing.

"Did you decide on tabletop decorations?" That had
been an intense debate to walk into yesterday after practice.
They were all shouting and pointing at colors and prices and
... I'd quietly slipped back out.

"Yes. I got them all to agree to the simpler, cheaper idea
of mason jars with flowers that also double as gifts people can
take home."

"That's smart," I agreed with a nod.

"Thanks."

She shifted and set her hand on my cheek. "You should
go to sleep. You've got a big day tomorrow."

I turned and kissed her palm. "You're right, but we've
both been so busy that I haven't really had a chance to just
talk to you. I miss you even though I see you each day."

She kissed my chest and nodded. "I miss you, too. One
great thing is that, no matter what happens in the game
tomorrow, we'll have more time together."

"That is a great thing," I agreed.

She patted my chest and rolled over. "Now, go to sleep so
you're well-rested for the game."

"Yes, ma'am."

She shuddered against me and said, "I love it when your
southern drawl comes out."

"You're not helping me go to sleep," I teased and nuzzled my nose against her neck.

She swatted at me. "Sleep! Sleep!"

Laughing, I rolled over so I wouldn't give into my impulses. "Yes, ma'am."

The morning and early afternoon passed in a blur of mechanical movements as I prepared for the final game. The final game of the season and of my career.

Porter thought I'd be sad about that fact, but it was honestly ... a relief.

Suited up and ready to go, I sat with headphones on, letting the music drown out the chatter of my teammates.

Porter sat beside me, his headphones on and some motivational speech playing in them. He tried to get me to listen to one, swearing it helped, but it had amped me up in an anxious way instead of an adrenaline way.

Coach came out and we all turned off our headphones and put them away to listen to his speech.

He looked at each of us, then focused on me and said, "Let's make this the best game we've ever played. Leave it all on the ice. Yeah?"

We all cheered and got off the bench, patting each other on the back and jumping from skate to skate as we pumped each other up. "Let's go!" we all shouted.

"Hands in!" Coach ordered.

We stuck our hands in, forming a circle around him, and cheered, "Ravens!"

Out on the ice, I could feel my smile stretching my face. Yeah, this was going to be a great game.

Looking up at the box, I raised my arm, pointed at Mollie where she stood, a huge matching smile on her face. Pounding my hand against my chest, I pointed back at her and then blew her a kiss.

She pretended to catch it and made a heart with her hands.

Porter and Brit did their own thing while the cameramen put us all up on the screen, a ritual of sorts by now.

My anxiety about her being in danger was negated thanks to the guards Porter had paid to stay in the box with them. Mollie had grumbled about it, trying to convince us that nothing had happened with Tiffany or anyone else, but finally gave up when Brit reminded her this was about the other team as well.

The game started and I had never felt so good. I scored two goals in each of the first two periods.

"I think I was worried about your shoulder for nothing," Porter said as we sat on the bench during the intermission between the second and third period, the final period.

I patted his shoulder and said, "Look at that! You can admit when you're wrong. I'm proud of you, Cap!"

He swatted my hand away, but we both continued smiling.

The buzzer sounded and we skated back out, bumping forearms as we got into position.

As the final period started, I knew something was different. The other team was much more vicious. They slammed

Porter into the glass twice, making him so angry he started to remove his gear to fight, but we stopped him.

As I neared their goal, ready to score again, two defenders slammed into me, bouncing me off the glass. My shoulder screamed in pain and I tried my best to hide it.

Skating back down to try to get the puck back, two more followed on my tail. Turning to head back as Porter got control of the puck, I was met with the two defenders moving in opposite directions, spinning me around and then slammed me into the glass again.

Black started to cover my vision as the pain erupted in my shoulder and I fell to the ice. My head bounced off the ice, making my vision spin.

"Sam!" Mollie screamed from the glass.

I didn't know when she made her way down, but I looked up at her worried face, only to then be met with a skate to the face.

CHAPTER 49
Mollie

THE CROWD BOOED THE PLAYER WHO KICKED SAM IN THE face while he was down.

I couldn't focus on anything but his eyes rolling up into the back of his head and blood dripping from his nose to the ice.

Porter shoved the player away and a huge fight broke out.

Tanner stood over Sam, keeping the fight away from him while the medics skated out to check him out.

His arm was at a weird angle, but I was hoping it was just from him being unconscious. He'd taken a few really hard hits and it had been obvious as he fell to the ice that his shoulder was hurting a lot.

I wanted to skate out on that ice and put the player who'd kicked him in his place, to yell at the players who'd ganged up on him to spin him into the glass.

Instead, I made my way to the side where they'd carry Sam through to take him to get checked out.

The coach stopped me. "You can't come back right now, Mollie."

"Coach," I choked.

He set a hand on my shoulder. "Go back to your box and we'll get you once he's done with the doctors. We will update you as we learn anything. You have to let the medics do their job."

I swallowed hard and nodded. "Okay."

He looked over my head at the guard who'd followed me. "Take her to the box. Don't let anyone in. We'll call on the line."

Watching Sam be carried off the ice on a stretcher made the tears I'd been fighting fall.

The guard set his hand on my shoulder and said, "Come on, Miss West. Let's get you back to the box where you'll be safe until we hear from the doctors."

A little girl stepped out of the row she'd been sitting in and handed me a small travel-sized pack of tissues. "He'll be okay, Mollie. Tucker is tough."

Trying my best to smile at the girl, I nodded. "I know."

Once back in the box, I sat numbly next to Brit, who wrapped me in a hug and rubbed my arms silently.

We both knew words were useless right now.

She got up, only to return a second later with drinks for us.

The game restarted and we watched as the Westwood Ravens refused to let the other team advance at all. The buzzer sounded, announcing the Westwood Ravens as the winners of the championship.

The joy I should have felt was tainted too much with worry.

The phone rang, making us both jump in our seats.

One of the guards, the one who'd gone down to the glass

with me, answered and nodded a few times before hanging up and turning towards us.

I gripped Brit's hands, mine covered in sweat and my heart pounded in my chest.

"He regained consciousness shortly after being taken back, but they think he has a concussion. His nose is broken. His shoulder was out of socket and they think he has a muscle tear. They're going to take him to the hospital for further x-rays and possibly surgery. There's a car ready to take you, if you'd like to go to the hospital, or it will take you back to your apartment. What would you like to do?"

"Take me to the hospital, please," I said, and stood, gathering my things.

"Do you want me to come?" Brit asked.

I shook my head. "You and Porter should celebrate with the rest of the team. I'll text you updates so you can let the team know." After a quick hug, I followed the guard out of the box where four more guards waited.

"They're going to help us get through the crowds," he explained.

I nodded my understanding and clutched my bag close. Once in the car, I sent a message to Marie and Sam's mom.

"Can we make one stop before the hospital?" I requested.

The guard nodded. "Want to pick up supplies?"

"Yes."

He smiled and said, "My mom was in the hospital a lot, so I understand. I'll let the driver know. There's a good store on the way that has lots of good snacks as well as healthy ones at good prices. They also sell blankets that fold up into a pillow, which I highly recommend."

"Thank you."

We made it to the vehicle after dodging cameras and reporters and they quickly ushered me into the car and on my way.

CHAPTER 50

Sam

WAKING UP IN THE HOSPITAL EVEN WHEN YOU KNOW you were sent there is always disorienting.

It was made better when I felt Mollie's hand in mine and saw her lying next to my hips, snoring softly with a bright blue blanket draped over her shoulders.

My entire body, including my face, felt tight and sore.

A nurse walked in and smiled at me. She checked my vitals then looked down at Mollie tenderly. "She's been by your side for two days non-stop. Even Porter couldn't convince her to step away."

"T-Two days?" I asked, my voice hoarse and dry.

The nurse held out a cup of water with a straw and I took a few sips. She nodded. "You had surgery and a reaction to the sedatives. Thankfully, you pulled through just fine. The doctor will be in shortly to check on you." She checked the IV drip and added, "You've been on painkillers, too, so if you feel drowsy, that's likely why. Push his button if the pain is unbearable."

Looking down, I realized that my shoulder was wrapped in a ton of white gauze.

I remembered everything up until I blacked out, so I'd figured they would need to do something to my arm, but it seemed more extensive than I'd anticipated. What surgery had they done?

The doctor came in and to my surprise, spoke quietly enough and moved slowly enough not to disturb Mollie. He explained my injuries and what they'd had to do.

Mollie woke up during his explanation and her grip on my hand tightened when she realized I was awake, but she didn't interrupt the doctor.

He also described what my recovery would be like and promised Mollie that they would write everything down for her before she could even ask.

When he left, she looked up at me and asked, "How do you feel?"

"Sore," I admitted.

"Pain?"

"No."

She exhaled and sank back down to rest her head on the hospital bed. "Thank goodness."

Porter and Brit walked in, both smiling when they found me awake.

"About time, Sleeping Beauty," Brit teased. "You've had our girl worried sick."

"Sorry," I said, and squeezed her hand.

Mollie went to the bathroom, giving me time to speak to Porter. "The game?" I asked.

He sat down and patted my knee. "We won, Champ! All thanks to you! You won MVP, too."

My eyes widened. "Seriously?"

He arched a brow. "You think I'd lie or joke about that?"

No, he definitely wouldn't.

"It was definitely one hell of a way to go out," Porter teased.

"You definitely went out on top," Brit said and chuckled.

I relaxed and exhaled softly. It was such a weight off my shoulders to know we'd won even if I hadn't witnessed the final parts of the game.

"How does it feel?" Porter asked as he took an apple slice that Brit had begun slicing up.

"Freeing," I admitted.

"Good," Brit said. "Now you can focus on planning the honeymoon."

"I'm surprised that wasn't your first order of business," I teased.

Mollie returned and took the apple slices Brit offered her, munching on them with bags beneath her eyes. "I wouldn't let them discuss it until we got the important parts of the wedding planned."

"And we all voted that you should be in charge of it," Brit said. "Since we're doing most of the other things."

"Wait, isn't today your wedding dress appointment?" I asked, realizing that two days had passed.

Mollie nodded. "I should call and reschedule."

"Nonsense," Porter said and stood. "You and Brit go. I'll stay here and keep Tucker company while he starts researching destinations for your honeymoon."

Mollie scowled, but I quickly said, "Go! You've been

needing to try on dresses and I want to surprise you with the honeymoon location anyway."

"Fine," she said, and Brit fist pumped the air.

"Do you have a passport?" I asked.

Mollie frowned at me. "Yeah?"

"Why did you answer my question with a question?" I teased.

"Come on," Brit rushed Mollie. "We've got to get your hair and makeup done before we go."

"What? Why?" Mollie asked as Brit grabbed their bags and dragged her towards the door.

"So you'll know for sure when you try on the dress that it's the one you want."

"Make sure he asks for meds if he's in pain! Don't let him tough it out," Mollie yelled over her shoulder.

"Will do," Porter called back. When the door shut behind them, he turned and smiled at me. "So, are you thinking more the Bahamas or Italy? I suggest Greece, personally."

CHAPTER 51

Mollie

WHILE BRIT DID MY HAIR, I ATE SOME RAMEN AND A boiled egg. The hospital hadn't been awful for eating, thanks to the driver stopping so I could pick things up, and Brit and Porter bringing me food, too.

However, nothing beat a fresh, hot, seasoned bowl of noodles prepared at home.

"Chew, girl. You're going to choke."

"Breaking news, a woman chokes on noodles," I said as I slurped up more.

Brit snorted and shook her head. "Dork."

"Marie messaged and asked you to take the large tablet so you can video call her to show off the dresses I'm trying on," I informed her.

Brit nodded. "Already planned on it and have it packed, plus snacks just in case, since I know you weren't eating well due to your stress waiting for Tucker to wake up."

She wasn't wrong. I'd been barely eating, mostly going through the motions when she or Porter forced me to. Or when the nurses would wake me up to drink water, threatening to put me on an IV drip if I didn't comply.

Once I finished eating, Brit did my makeup, but wouldn't let me see my reflection before hurrying me out to her car and to the dress shop.

A tall, fit, brunette woman in a skintight burgundy dress met us as soon as we entered, two glasses of champagne on a tray in one hand. "Hello, Miss West. Welcome to our shop. I am Jasmine. If you'll follow me, we'll get you started on your magical journey of choosing *the* dress." She had a slight accent, possibly French, that made her sound regal.

I exchanged a look with Brit, surprised by the seemingly VIP treatment, which only grew as we were led to a private area with a raised dais surrounded by mirrors. There was a couch behind it for Brit to sit on and she immediately set up the tablet, calling Marie.

Once I set my bag down, Jasmine handed me my glass of champagne and smiled wide. "From the answers you provided on our quiz, we've placed a few dresses in the room for you to begin trying on. We will select others, if necessary, once you try these on and tell us your likes and dislikes. I will be right here, outside this curtain, to step in and zip, lace, and tighten things up when you've got the dress on."

I nodded, feeling a bit out of my comfort zone with all of this. "Okay."

"There's a shelf inside for you to set your glass down while you change clothes," Jasmine said as she pulled the curtain back for me to step inside the dressing room.

Once the curtain closed behind me, I silently chastised myself for feeling uncomfortable. I was trying on dresses, not walking down the aisle!

Knowing Brit and Marie would harass me if I didn't hurry, I took a quick drink of my champagne, set it down, and stripped my clothes, setting them on the chair by the curtain.

One thing I immediately noticed was the lack of mirrors in this room. You couldn't look at yourself until you stepped out onto the dais.

Facing the dresses that hung up, my eyes widened as I took in the gorgeous white gowns.

One gown had a tulle skirt and tulle on the bodice that called to me, and I quickly put that one on.

"I'm ready for you to zip me," I announced.

Jasmine stepped in and zipped me up, checking me over before opening the curtain and picking up the train. "After you."

Eyes on the floor so I didn't trip as I walked up to the two steps to the dais, I waited to raise my eyes until Jasmine had fluffed out the train and arranged the front my dress.

"You can open your eyes now," she whispered and I could hear the smile in her voice before I even opened my eyes to see it in place.

Looking behind her, I gasped as I looked at my reflection.

Was it my reflection? Was that really ... me?

"Oh, no. I'm already crying," Marie sobbed.

"It's beautiful," Brit said on a sigh.

It was. It was more beautiful than I could have imagined. The tulle on the bodice made the dress.

"Take pictures," Jasmine ordered Brit. "She will want to look at the pictures again before deciding which dress to select. Trust me. I've been in this business for twenty years."

I looked at the women in the mirror and said, "Did you start as a toddler?"

She laughed and waved at me while blushing. "You flatter me. Do you have any dislikes of this dress?"

I shook my head. "None at all."

She nodded, smiling like she had expected that answer and said, "Come, let's have you try on another dress."

CHAPTER 52

Sam

PORTER QUICKLY LIVED UP TO HIS BEST MAN STATUS. Not only was he a huge help when it came to picking the hotel and flights for our honeymoon, but he even chipped in for part of it and let me use some of his miles.

I had turned him down at first, but he was adamant and threatened to steal my computer to do it anyway.

Then, he planned and threw the most epic bachelor party that followed in line with my tastes and preferences. So, it wasn't like the crazy parties you saw in movies, but that's not what I'd wanted, and Porter had known that. I wasn't one hundred percent recovered yet, which also meant I didn't get as crazy as I could have.

Brit and Marie had tried to get Mollie to go to Vegas for her bachelorette party, but she opted instead for a local one, so she could invite some of her ice skating friends, Alicia included.

Mollie and I sat on the couch, completely exhausted, and mentally preparing for our trip home for our wedding. It was the lull before the storm, as she called it. My mom called

Marie and Brit at least three times a day to check on things and while they were handling most things, I knew the entire thing was starting to wear Mollie out. She'd spent three full days going over the wedding registry, but we quickly realized we didn't need any of the items. So, she put a bolded, all caps note at the top of our registry site that we didn't need items and if they felt adamantly about giving, that they could donate to our honeymoon spending fund.

Truthfully, we were both ready to have the wedding and move on to the best part, the honeymoon.

"Only a couple more days until you're legally mine," I teased her and pulled her so she leaned back against my chest, her butt and legs between my legs.

She set her hand on my arm that lay around her waist and said, "I'm pretty sure that's my line."

I squeezed her and sighed happily. "It's hard to believe I got this second chance with my adorable, nerdy, high school crush and she became a smokin' hot librarian to exceed all of my fantasies."

"Well, I'm super lucky, because my high school crush became one of the top players in college hockey and has a set of abs I could wash my clothes on." Laughing she added, "Though I think the town might not appreciate such a display. It might make the little old ladies faint."

"We'd definitely be the talk of the town then," I said and kissed the top of her head.

"It's already going to be annoying how much attention we're going to get. I don't want to add any additional reasons to gain more." She huffed and I laughed.

"My poor little wallflower. I'm sorry you've gained so much notoriety being my girlfriend, and soon, wife."

"Do you think anyone will recognize us in Greece? Probably not, right? Good."

I hadn't even had the opportunity to respond before she answered herself.

"We should get to bed," she said and sighed. "Our flight will be here before we know it."

"You're right," I agreed and started to pick her up as I leaned forward to stand, but she rolled away from me and narrowed her eyes.

"You're not allowed to pick me up yet, remember? Your shoulder is still healing."

I rolled my eyes. "Mollie, I'm fine. I'm not well enough to play contact sports, but if you recall, I'm not doing that any longer. Picking you up is nothing."

I tried to reach for her again, but she scrambled off the couch and held her hand out. "No! I'm not letting you injure yourself right before our honeymoon!"

Okay, she did have a point there. I wanted to be ready for whatever happened on our honeymoon.

"Fine," I said, and sighed in defeat.

She nodded and hurried into bed, wrapping the front of the covers tight around her front, cocooning her inside. If I weren't climbing in behind her, she would have become a little Mollie blanket burrito.

It was pretty adorable when she did it.

Sliding in beneath the covers, I spooned my larger body around hers, my hand stroking down her thigh before sliding up to wrap around her stomach. "I love you, Mollie."

"I love you, too, Sam. I can't wait to be Mrs. Tucker."

"And I can't wait to carry you across the threshold of your house," I whispered.

She shivered against me. "That southern charm of yours is quite sexy when you let it out."

"Only for you, baby."

She laughed softly. "Better keep it that way, Mr. Tucker."

"Yes, ma'am," I agreed and kissed the side of her neck.

CHAPTER 53

Mollie

"I'm sweating more than Jezebel in church," Ms. Tucker said, fanning herself with the foldable fan she'd brought for the ceremony.

The day was warmer than expected, but I was also stressed and nervous.

Marie flicked the spot between my brows, above my nose. "Stop scowling. Everything is ready and all you have to do is smile, walk down the aisle, say 'I do,' and enjoy your future as Mrs. Mollie Tucker."

Brit set a floor fan down, plugged it in, and aimed it at both Ms. Tucker and I. "Sweating in your dresses is not ideal for pictures."

"Have the men finished their pictures?" Marie asked Brit.

She nodded. "Yep. The photographer is on her way over here to take ours next."

The events and time flew by as I took pictures, freshened makeup and hair, sipped on water, and tried to calm my racing heart.

Mrs. Tucker went to take her seat at the front where the mother of the groom would sit, giving me a tight hug and a warm smile. "I can't wait to have you as my daughter officially."

I would not cry. I would not ruin my makeup.

"Thank you," I said, hugging her again.

Once she was gone, I went back to stressing about the huge crowd and cameras that awaited me.

"Girl, take a drink of this," Brit ordered and handed me a glass of champagne.

"Where did you get this?" I asked as I hadn't even seen her open it.

"I knew you were going to be stressing, so I brought it just in case." She poured herself and Marie a glass as well and held her cup out. "To you for being the most beautiful bride."

Marie and I hit our plastic cups against hers and then I gulped my glass down.

I wasn't having second thoughts, not a point zero zero zero zero zero one percent chance of that. The nervousness was from walking down the aisle and standing before so many people.

Our small town, backyard wedding had become so large that we had to change venues, and not to Mrs. Delaney's barn or the senior center. No, we were getting married in the gazebo in the center of the town square. The entire town would be shut down, no driving in, through, or out of town since we had chairs placed in a circle around the gazebo, out into the street, in front of the businesses that formed the square, and there were going to be many with standing room only as well.

The news outlets had heard about the wedding and were coming, too.

They were treating us like we were celebrities, which was a bit insane, but apparently, I'd gained followers and fans from how I had supported Sam during his games. My social media followers were in the thousands, despite me only posting random photos very rarely.

I didn't understand it at all, but it meant the wedding was huge now and the news was covering it, so it increased my anxiety tenfold.

We were in a room inside of City Hall, since it was closest to the gazebo, and I could walk out the front doors and straight to the gazebo. Brit had insisted on finding a red carpet for me to walk down and I loved it, even if I was hesitant to admit that verbally.

Raising my arms, I let the fan blow on my armpits, which were starting to sweat.

"Alright, time to go," Marie said, checked my makeup and hair again, then began to bundle up my dress's train into her arms.

Brit grabbed my bouquet and Marie's, holding hers and Marie's in one hand since mine was much thicker than theirs.

We moved from the room and out to the main doors. Our heels clacked loudly on the tile in the silent City Hall. Two security officers, a pair of older gentlemen who had been guards here almost as long as I'd been alive, stood at the doors, big smiles on their faces. "Congratulations, Mollie. We're so proud of everything you're doing and know you and Sammy will be happy together," Mr. Stanson, the guard on the left, said.

"Thank you, Mr. Stanson," I replied and felt some of my anxiety lessen. It was funny how a simple gesture like that could help so much. Taking a deep breath, I took my bouquet from Marie and nodded. "I'm ready."

CHAPTER 54

Sam

THERE HAD BEEN A TON OF WORK UP TO TODAY, BUT I had thought the wedding day itself wouldn't be as hectic and stressful.

Boy was I wrong.

After the venue change, the late night reorganization meetings, shipments missing, rush store runs, and more things, I was tired.

There were things that had happened that we hadn't told Mollie about since she'd been incredibly overwhelmed as it was. For instance, our original DJ came down with the flu, so we'd had to find a replacement, which thankfully was easy to do since Triston, one of our teammates, was a DJ for fun and was already planning to come. I'd offered to pay him, but he said it was really a gift to him to get to DJ for my wedding.

Our photoshoot before the wedding took longer than planned due to the coach and team barging in and forcing us to take more pictures with them as well. I had obliged since I wouldn't be back next season. Coach had even made me tear up and hugged me.

Three news outlets were set up on the outer edge of the guests, their cameras pointed at the gazebo where I sat, waiting for the wedding to start.

Mom walked over, fanning herself with her favorite foldable fan that had a painting of a weeping willow on it Dad had gotten her before he died. She sat in her assigned chair and waved me over.

Squatting down, I set my hand on her knee and smiled up at the woman who had raised me. "How are you doing, Mama?"

She patted my cheek gently and smiled wide. "Your wife looks absolutely gorgeous. Though, I can tell she's a bit nervous about coming out here in front of so many people."

I laughed softly. "Can't say I'm surprised to hear that. My little librarian prefers to hide in the back, rather than being seen at the front."

Nodding, she said, "I was surprised at first when I heard you were dating her, but you two make a lovely couple and she is a great woman. You better do right by her and treat her like a queen, you hear me? You're not too old to get smacked with a newspaper if you do something wrong."

Laughing again, I patted her knee. "I'll be the best gentleman ever."

"You get all checked in for your flights?" she asked.

"Yep. Thank goodness for phone apps. I did it between the photoshoot and now." I had cut it close, too, but thankfully, we were both checked in and ready to fly out of the country.

"You two better bring me back some souvenirs," she ordered. "A shot glass at the very least."

"Yes, ma'am," I said and stood.

The pastor, the only one in our town, who had been with the church here for forty years, hobbled up in a pair of white slacks and a white button-up shirt. He smiled at Mom and then turned to me. "You ready, son?"

I nodded. "Yes, sir."

He hobbled up the steps and sat on the bench that lined the inside of the gazebo. "Good. Good. This is one heck of a wedding. Largest our town has ever seen."

"It definitely got larger than we anticipated." I laughed softly and shrugged. "Not that I'm complaining."

He winked. "Course not."

Porter approached and said, "Guests are going to be led into their seats now. Stay inside this gazebo. Mollie is just about ready, so once they're seated, we will start the ceremony."

Taking a deep breath, I smiled at him and asked, "You have the rings?"

Patting his jacket pocket, he nodded. "I've only checked like three dozen times in the last ten minutes."

We both laughed and got into place. Me, hiding inside the gazebo with the pastor, him going to help the volunteers seat people.

Dropping my head down, I closed my eyes, and tried to block out the sounds of the guests. It wasn't that I was being antisocial, but once some of these older men and women started talking, they rarely stopped.

It took forty minutes for the guests to get seated even with the stellar work of our volunteers.

Finally, the time came and I took my spot in the center of the gazebo, hands clasped in front of me, waiting for Mollie to walk down the literal red carpet.

Porter dusted off my jacket, adjusted some of my hair on my forehead, winked, and stepped back to my left.

The City Hall's main doors opened and a goddess stepped out, the sun reflecting around her, making her glow, and her eyes found mine immediately.

I sucked in a breath and Porter whistled softly beside me.

"Mine," I breathed.

He snickered, but we both silenced when the pastor gave us a look.

Mollie walked down the City Hall steps, her eyes focused on mine, and I felt my heart flutter like it had when I'd seen her for our first date, but like ten times as powerful.

How the hell had I gotten so lucky as to gain the attention of a goddess personified?

CHAPTER 55
Mollie

Sam's eyes widened when he saw me and stayed glued to me the entire time I walked down the red carpet, our aisle, and up to the gazebo.

A small sense of smug satisfaction coursed through me at his reaction.

Keeping my eyes focused on him was easy. He looked sexy and handsome in his fitted tuxedo, a small daisy in his pocket to match my bouquet.

As I stepped up into the gazebo, he grabbed my hand, pulled me forward, and whispered, "I didn't realize I was marrying a goddess."

My cheeks flushed at the compliment. "Sam," I whispered.

Marie took my bouquet while Brit spread out my train.

The pastor began his speech and I continued to stare up into Sam's eyes while he held my hands and rubbed his thumb over the back of my hand.

I was the luckiest woman in the world.

The fact that a small town, nerdy, little librarian like me

was marrying not just her school crush, but *the* Sam Tucker ... insane.

After our vow exchange and the exchange of rings, Sam slipped an arm around my waist, dipped me, and kissed me so thoroughly that I was pretty sure I could combust at any time.

We straightened and he linked our hands so we could walk side by side down the red carpet, waving to our friends, family, and the media.

Porter made the announcement for all the guests to head to the reception site.

Sam and I made our way to City Hall where we would wait for the guests to leave, then take pictures at the gazebo before heading to the reception. The guests would have appetizers and drinks to tide them over until we arrived.

Once the doors of City Hall closed behind us, Sam spun me around into his arms and hugged me tight. "You're officially mine, Mrs. Mollie Tucker. I'm the luckiest man on the planet."

I rested my face against his jacket and laughed softly as I looked at my sparkling emerald wedding ring. "It's the best feeling."

He kissed my cheek while squeezing me tight. "It is."

"Hey, don't ruin her makeup. We've got pictures to take," Marie chastised.

"Here's some water," Brit said, and handed us both a water bottle.

Porter opened the front doors and leaned just his head inside. "Time for pictures."

After we took our pictures, Marie and Brit bustled my dress and we made our way to the reception site, where tents had been set up with tables and chairs and we ate and laughed with our friends and family.

It was everything I had dreamed a wedding could be and so much more, because I did it with my best friend, my new husband.

Sam and I danced a ton and by the end of the night, my feet were sore, but my heart was full.

Porter surprised us with a limo waiting at the end of the reception to take us to one of the neighboring cities to a fancy hotel, where we had a jacuzzi tub in the hotel room and champagne waiting for us.

Sam and I soaked in the jacuzzi tub, bubbles up to our chests, each holding a glass of champagne.

"I'm definitely buying a spa for the house," I said with my eyes closed, resting my head back. The hot water and jets were perfect for relaxing after such a busy day.

"I agree," Sam said. "We definitely need a spa. We'll have to get a big one though, because I have a feeling that we'll have company over often."

I laughed softly. "Most likely."

"So, Mrs. Tucker," he whispered, his hands sliding up from my knees to my upper thighs. "What do you say we rinse off in the shower real quick and consummate this marriage?"

I opened my eyes and stared into his, my lower body molten, and nodded. "Yes, please."

He picked me up and stepped out of the tub, setting me on my feet inside the shower, placing kisses along my neck and shoulders.

Turning on the water, we both yelped and jumped to opposite sides of the shower as cold water sprayed us.

Immediately, we both dissolved into a fit of laughter, looking at each other from across the water.

He stepped forward at the same time I did, hands grabbing and pulling each other flush together under the now steaming water. "I love you, Mollie."

"I love you, too, Sam. Forever."

He nodded. "Forever."

CHAPTER 56
Sam

THE WARM SAND BETWEEN MY TOES, THE SUN ON MY skin, and the sound of the waves crashing against the beach combined were the most relaxing thing I'd ever experienced in my life.

Having Mollie laying on a towel next to me in a sexy white bikini made it even better. My adorable wife – man I loved being able to think of her as that – lay on the towel on her stomach, her feet kicking back and forth as she read a book. Occasionally, she would reach over, pick up her margarita, and take a drink.

Honestly, I could watch her like this all day every day and die a happy man.

Her stomach suddenly grumbled and she paused kicking her feet. "Um, can we get food soon?"

Snickering softly, I asked, "What would you like to eat?"

"You pick."

We both knew she just didn't know what to order here since she didn't speak the language. Even though I assured her that the hotel staff spoke English, she felt awkward ordering from them.

"I'll be right back," I said and stood.

She gave me a thumbs up without looking away from her book.

As I walked away, I thought about her ex-boyfriend and how he most definitely would have been upset that she wanted to read on the honeymoon. How she wouldn't have done it to make him happy. I was so glad that she was with me and could be her authentic self. Who cared if she wanted to read? I was enjoying the view and napping, so why should I care if she read while I did that?

Honestly, the people watching was pretty good here. I'd caught her peeking from over the top of her book to watch people occasionally.

Grabbing my satchel that held my wallet, passport, and some local currency, I headed away from the water and to our hotel's café just at the edge of the beach. This resort was amazing and I was extremely grateful that Porter had known about it.

I would have to do something nice for him to repay him.

"Two orders of your special," I said as I got my turn to order. "Oh, and two more margaritas."

Leaning my elbows on the counter, I waited for my order to be made.

A familiar face headed towards me and fear rippled through me a moment as Tiffany approached with an unfamiliar man on her arm.

"Wow, what a small world! I didn't expect to see you here, Tucker. Where's your lovely wife?" she asked.

Her entire demeanor was pleasant and completely different than the last times we'd seen her.

"Uh, she's on the beach," I answered vaguely. "What are you doing here?"

She squeezed the arm of the man and said, "Antoine and I are here on vacation."

He held out his hand and smiled. "Nice to meet you, Mr. Tucker. I'm a big fan. I wasn't a big hockey fan before, but Tiff convinced me to watch the finals and you played one hell of a game."

"Thank you," I said, and returned his smile.

"I wanted to apologize about all that stuff that happened before," she said softly, her eyes dropping as she looked sad. "I was in a bad place and I'm really sorry. I wish I could take it all back. I don't expect you to forgive me, but if you could tell Mollie, I, uh, I don't have the courage to face her. Anyway. Nice to see you. Enjoy your honeymoon!"

Before I could even respond, she turned and the two of them walked away, down the beach and towards the neighboring resort.

Wow. I was glad that she was in a better place, but so surprised that I couldn't really wrap my head around the interaction that had just happened.

I guess everyone really did deserve a second chance and an opportunity to grow.

"Your order, sir," the café employee said in a thick accent.

I turned and smiled as I accepted the bag and two drinks. "Thank you so much. Have a great day."

As I made my way across the warm sand, I debated if I should tell Mollie. It wasn't that I wanted to hide it from her, but I worried she might stress out and feel scared if she saw Tiffany here.

But if she saw Tiffany before I said anything, it would definitely freak her out even more.

Should I wait until later, let her enjoy the rest of the afternoon first?

"Your food has arrived, my queen," I said as I made it to our chairs and the towel where she still lay reading.

She put her bookmark in her book and popped up so fast that it startled me and made me take a step back.

Her brows furrowed. "You okay?"

Exhaling, I set the drinks and food down on the little table next to the umbrella and said, "I have something to tell you, but I need you to stay calm until I finish the entire explanation."

She frowned heavily, but sat in the chair and nodded. "Okay."

I told her everything about the encounter and while her eyebrows rose and her eyes widened, she remained quiet through my full recounting.

After a beat of silence, she smiled and said, "Well, I hope the guy she's with is good to her and she's really happy."

Now it was my turn to frown. "What?"

Shrugging, she opened the container of her food and said, "We all change and grow, right? Sometimes it takes a bad experience to necessitate that positive change. You and I aren't exactly the same people we were when we started dating, right?"

"Right."

She smiled and asked, "Were you worried I would freak out and get paranoid?"

I sat and exhaled loudly. "Honestly, yeah."

Patting my hand, she held out my margarita to me. "I think you can thank Brit and Porter for my more relaxed nature. Although they were both paranoid about Tiffany previously, they also instilled the importance of living in the moment and being prepared, but also not so nervous you can't enjoy the moment. It took me a bit to fully understand, but I think I've finally grasped it."

My eyes widened and I realized I owed Porter more than I knew.

"That's honestly great to hear. I need to learn to do that a bit more myself."

She chuckled and leaned over to kiss my cheek. "Yes, you do, husband."

I slid a hand around the back of her neck and kept her from pulling away, staring into her slightly widened eyes, I whispered, "Say that again."

"Husband," she said in a breathy, sexy voice.

I moaned and kissed her hard, our tongues tangling together briefly before I pulled back. Her cheeks had reddened and she smiled at me. "I love hearing you say that."

"I enjoy saying it, but I need to eat or I'm about to be hangry." She kissed the tip of my nose and I reluctantly released my hold on the back of her neck.

"Fine, but only because I don't want you hangry and breathing fire to melt the sand into glass."

She rolled her eyes. "If I could breathe fire, it wouldn't be to melt the sand."

"Oh, what would you use your fire breath for?"

"Evil, duh," she said and cackled maniacally.

Leaning over, I kissed her cheek again. "I always knew you preferred villainous men."

Nodding, she said, "Heroes can be celibate. I want that man who would burn down the world to save their woman. Not the one who would sacrifice her for the world. Plus, I have a feeling that the villain would be a better lover too."

"Oh, why is that?"

"Because he knows what it's like to be left out to dry, dismissed by others, and he wouldn't do that to his lover."

I leaned closer and asked, "So, do you want me to play a villain tonight, wife?"

She swallowed hard and nodded. "Yes, please."

"Your wish is my command," I said and kissed her on the tip of her nose.

She let out a shaky breath. "Tease."

Snickering, I pushed her drink towards her. "I think it's your turn to take a drink."

"There's not enough liquid in this world to make me less thirsty for you, Sam Tucker."

"Alright, that's it, lunch is cancelled. We're going to the hotel room."

I picked her up over my shoulder, making her laugh and squeal, but she smacked my back and said, "No! Bad! You have to wait until I finish my food and drink."

I set her down and said, "Fine, but make it fast."

She looked me dead in the eye and said, "That's *not* what she said." Immediately, she threw her head back and laughed, clutching her stomach as she cracked herself up.

I shook my head and laughed as well. "You're such a dork."

"But I'm your dork," she said and winked, or tried to, but sand got in her eye and she ended up bent over wiping at her face.

Yes, she was mine alright. All mine.

CHAPTER 57

Mollie

TWO YEARS LATER

Brit hugged me tight, her grip bruising, but I simply hugged her back.

"It's not forever, Brit. We'll see you for Thanksgiving," I reminded her.

She sniffled. "I don't want you to go!"

"You're going back to your hometown as well," I said and laughed softly, patting her back.

"It's not fair. I want to see you every day like Marie gets to."

"Well, you'd have to live near me for that, which would be impossible with Porter's NHL career." We were all thrilled for him getting drafted and he definitely deserved it. I had no doubt he'd be one of the top players very quickly.

"You promise we'll videocall?" she asked as she reluctantly released me. "Every week?"

I nodded. "As often as you want."

"And you're coming to us for Christmas, right?"

I nodded again. "Yep."

Grabbing a tissue, she blew her nose and said, "Okay."

Sam slid an arm around my waist and pulled me back against his chest. "I can have my wife back now?"

Brit narrowed her eyes. "For now."

Porter pulled me away from Sam and hugged me, sniffling, too. "I changed my mind. You come with us instead. I'll buy you all the books you want."

Sam punched Porter's shoulder. "Give me my wife!"

"No, you're too selfish," Porter said and hugged me tighter.

I shook my head. "You and Brit are going to see us in five months. It's not that long."

"It's forever!" he shouted, but after a shuddering breath, he released me and immediately pulled Sam into a hug. "Don't go, Tuck!"

"You two are so dramatic," Sam sighed.

"Whatever, Mr. No-Heart!" Brit accused.

"You know our house is always open for you," I reminded them. "You need a weekend away, just hop on a plane and come see us."

"I'm going to take you up on that offer," Brit said.

"For sure," Porter agreed and let Sam go.

"You have all your bags?" Brit asked. "The apartment is all cleaned out?"

"Yes, Mollie went over it like six times," Sam answered.

"You sure you don't want us to give you a ride to the airport?" Porter asked.

"You have your own events tonight. Your family is taking

you out to dinner in two hours, remember?" His parents were so proud of him for being drafted and were pulling out all the stops to praise him.

"Right. Right," he agreed.

I gave him and Brit one more hug before climbing into our rental car. Sam had sold his car, saying he wasn't attached to it and if we needed more than one vehicle, we'd buy another at that time. So, when we'd returned for our graduation ceremony and to clean out his apartment, we'd opted to just rent a car until we left. "We'll call you when we land," I promised.

"You better," Porter said.

"And videocall Saturday," Brit reminded me.

"You got it," Sam said and climbed into the passenger seat.

We waved as we drove away and I felt my shoulders slump a bit.

Sam set his hand on my leg and said, "It's always hard to leave a place you've been at for so long."

"It was only a few years, but I really enjoyed college and this city," I agreed.

"But it's going to be even better finally living full time in your beautiful house and being Director of the library!"

I smiled wide at the reminder. As soon as I finished my last class, I'd put in my application for Director. Surprisingly, they hadn't replaced Tanya Smith, the former Director, after firing her. Even more surprising was getting a call two days after submitting my application to let me know that I'd gotten the position and was expected to start in just a few weeks. They were also paying me more than they'd paid Tanya, which made me feel a little bit vindicated.

"I can't wait to start instituting all the improvement plans I've got prepared. I'm going to be super busy the next few months."

He patted my leg and said, "I've got my own hands full at my uncle's place. The marketing plan I've got in mind is very aggressive and I've got high hopes for it."

"I'm sure it's going to do well." I squeezed his hand and turned to smile at him.

Although it wasn't exactly what he'd had planned for himself, he was truly happy with the job, something I'd been worried about initially, thinking he was settling for me, but that couldn't be farther from the truth.

"Oh, when is that skating training camp?" Sam asked.

I rolled my eyes. "In four weeks. It's been on our calendar for months, Sam."

"Right. Right. The shared calendar."

"You never open it, do you?"

He flinched. "Busted."

Laughing and shaking my head, I said, "Well, some things never change."

"Are you going to participate in the tournament in December? That big open one?" he asked.

"As long as I'm making consistent progress in my routine and I think I'm prepared, yes. I've got enough time, that I don't think it will be a problem."

Skating had become a big part of my life and I was glad that even after the attack and breaking my leg, that I was able to continue doing it. Not everyone was so lucky.

"Are you excited about the teen hockey camp?" I asked. Sam had decided to offer a hockey camp for teens in our hometown during the summer. So far, over fifteen kids, both male and female, had signed up.

"I'm up to twenty kids now!" he exclaimed.

"Whoa, that's awesome, babe!"

"Porter is going to stop by for one of the days, which is going to be really exciting for the kids."

I smiled and said, "I'm pretty sure they're already excited to get to be taught by the famous Samuel Tucker."

"I'm not that famous," he muttered.

At the airport, it took us quite a bit of time to return the car, check our bags, and get through security. We ended up jogging through the airport to catch our flight.

Once seated, I tucked my blanket around myself and put my eye mask on so I could take a nap.

I knew we'd have very little time before we were expected to visit Sam's mom.

"You ready?" Sam asked in a whisper as he linked his hand with mine.

"For?" I asked as I raised my eye mask to look at him.

"The next part of our life." He smiled wide.

My heart felt like it couldn't get any fuller. "As long as you're with me, yes."

He kissed the side of my head and said, "Good answer, Mrs. Tucker."

CHAPTER 58

Sam

"LEARNING TO STOP AND SKATE IN THE OPPOSITE direction is extremely important to learn to play hockey. If the puck gets stolen, you need to be able to stop and turn to chase after it. So, twenty sprints! Now!" I blew the whistle and the twenty-five kids pushed off, skating down the ice, to complete the drills.

The smile on my face hadn't dropped since I started the camp four days earlier. They were all so eager to learn, so excited to play, and thought I was a much bigger star than I was.

The real star would be arriving today.

My day job with my uncle's company was going great, but it was nice to have this week off to hold the hockey training camp for teenagers. I'd been shocked at first that girls had signed up, but they were just as good and just as motivated as the boys. There were a few of the players that I was definitely going to keep internet search alerts for because I knew they were going to go places in the hockey community.

"They look much better than the first day, I'm

impressed," Mollie commented as she leaned over the edge of the rink next to me.

I bent over to kiss her on the lips before straightening and focusing back on the kids. "Yeah, they're quick studies, for sure. How was work? Did the event go well?"

"It was good, we had about six kids show up for the read-along. I have to remind myself how small our town is and that I can't expect more kids to show than actually live here."

Laughing, I said, "Very true, love. Very true."

They finished their drills, so I blew the whistle again. "Alright, head over, hydrate, and remove your skates. I've got a surprise for you." Leaning over, I whispered, "He is here, right?"

She nodded while smiling wide. "You don't see the indentions in my arms from the hugs?"

Had it been any other man, I would have been jealous and seen red, but not with Porter. He was basically Mollie's brother at this point, and they even called each other brother and sister.

Mollie moved out of the way so the kids could use the door to get off the ice and they all greeted her warmly, her presence an almost constant as she brought snacks and visited often.

"You look lovely today, Mrs. Tucker," Trenton, one of the best players here, said.

She smiled. "Thank you, Trenton. You're looking good out there, a definite improvement even from yesterday. Are you sneaking in extra practices?"

His cheeks reddened. "Thank you, ma'am." With head down, he hurried off to get water.

My eyes narrowed slightly. Perhaps I needed to double check the security of the rink.

"I'll go fetch Porter," she whispered, kissed my cheek, and skipped up the stairs.

I watched her go and Trenton caught me staring. He gave me a knowing smile and turned back to talk to one of the girls in the camp.

"I've got a special surprise for you today, everyone. You've all been doing a great job this week, listening and putting what you're learning into practice. So, I'd like you to meet one of the men who helped shape me and my play style. He's a recently recruited NHL player, but I'm certain you've all heard of him. Everyone, Jackson Porter!"

Porter walked down the stairs, Brit and Mollie behind him, all three carrying large boxes. "Hello!" Porter greeted. "I'm so happy to be here. When my best friend told me about this camp, I knew I had to make room in my schedule to come by."

"Oh my god, he's even more handsome in person," one of the girls said, causing a few others to snicker and nod their heads.

"His girlfriend is gorgeous. Is she a model?" Trenton asked one of his guy friends.

I smiled, knowing if Brit had heard it would make her day. I'd tell her later tonight.

The kids surrounded Porter, getting autographs and pictures. I helped take the pictures on their cell phones and saw Brit and Mollie taking pictures for our advertising as well.

The boxes turned out to be NHL jerseys, pucks, towels, and a few other items.

"How'd you get all this?" I asked Brit as I made my way up the stairs to where she and Mollie were taking pictures.

"The NHL heard he was coming out here to visit you and what you were doing and donated them. We didn't even ask." She shrugged. "We figured it would make the kids happy."

They were all beaming, so that had definitely been true.

She threw her arms around me and hugged me tight. "Where's my hug, you brat?"

Laughing, I returned her hug and whispered in here ear what Trenton had asked.

As expected, she preened at that and said, "Maybe someday."

"Get back down there so you're in the pictures, too," Mollie ordered. "Have them ask questions."

"Oh, good idea," I praised, kissed her, and clapped my hands to get the kids' attention. "How about a little Q&A with Mr. Porter? Raise your hand if you've got a question for him."

Every single one of them raised their hands.

Porter and I laughed and we let them ask questions for the next hour. I was so grateful to have someone willing to stick around so long for a group of kids. I knew in the next few years, Porter wouldn't have this kind of time available, so I was happy he was doing it now.

After sending the kids home for the night, packing up what was left from the NHL items, and locking up, we walked through the town towards our house.

Brit inhaled loudly and exhaled even louder. "It's so clean smelling here. And so quiet."

Porter nodded and waved at a few older ladies who were

gawking at him. "I always love visiting here. Maybe when I retire, I'll move here, too."

"You just got drafted, don't be talking about retirement already," Mollie said and playfully smacked his arm.

He draped his arm around her shoulders and said, "Don't worry, Sis. I'm going to make a big name for myself and show the world how awesome I am first."

At the house, they each grabbed a beer before finding a place in the kitchen to hangout while Mollie cooked. It was a ritual we'd started while still in college and it made my chest warm to see it in Mollie and my home now.

Before anyone could see me tearing up like a baby, I snapped a picture and discreetly wiped my eyes. This may not have been the life fifteen-year-old Samuel Tucker had dreamed of, but dammit, this was exactly the life I wanted. I would do anything to protect this wonderful life.

"You okay, Sam?" Porter asked, holding out a beer for me, a knowing smile on his face.

I smiled, took the beer, kissed my wife atop her head, and said, "Yeah, I'm great."

For more romance, check out my other books at www. catherinebanks.com and join my newsletter at catbanks.co/ Newsletter

About the Author

Cathy Banks is the MF contemporary romance pseudonym for Catherine Banks, USA Today Bestselling Author.

amazon.com/author/daisyemory

About the Author

Catherine Banks is an award-winning, USA Today bestselling author who writes in several fantasy subgenres and has multiple pseudonyms. She began writing fiction at only four years old and finished her first full-length novel at the age of fifteen. She is married to her soulmate and best friend, Avery, who she has two amazing children with. After her full-time job, she reads books, plays video games, and watches anime shows and movies with her family to relax. Although she has lived in Northern California her entire life, she dreams of traveling around the world. Catherine is also C.E.O. of Turbo Kitten Industries™, a company with many hats including being a book publisher and Etsy store full of nerdy fun.

facebook.com/catherinebanksauthor

amazon.com/author/catherinebanks

bookbub.com/authors/catherine-banks